I0626312

A Zach and Zora Comic Mystery

BAD DAY IN A
BANANA HAMMOCK

STUART R. WEST

GORDIAN KNOT BOOKS

Copyright © 2015 by Stuart R. West
ISBN 978-1-63789-618-1
Gordian Knot is an imprint of Crossroad Press Publishing
All rights reserved. No part of this book may be used or reproduced in any manner whatsoever
without written permission except in the case of
brief quotations embodied in critical articles and reviews
For information address Crossroad Press at 141 Brayden Dr., Hertford, NC 27944
www.crossroadpress.com

Cover art and design by David Dodd

First Crossroad Press Edition - 2023

Dedication

This book goes out to my friend, Meradeth Houston, who dared me to write it. So blame her.

And to my loves, my family, Cydney and Sarah. Like Zach and Zora, together we can do anything.

Chapter One

Zach woke up with a slamming headache, the first thing that seemed a little off. But the dead man in bed next to him was way off. No recollection whatsoever how it happened, either.

Zach's stomach roiled at the implication.

But…but I'm not gay!

Tufts of gray hair stuck up from the dead man's head, a clown's perm. His eyes, glassy and milky, locked onto the ceiling. His mouth gaped open, a silent moan of horror. One arm perched over his head and his knuckles grazed the wall. Zach carefully pinched back the sheet.

Dammit. Yep, naked.

Revolted, he jumped out of bed, clad in nothing but his banana hammock. Dizziness swooped over him and the floor spun beneath his feet.

"Whoa."

Worn bedsprings crunched as he crashed back onto the bed. The dead man's hand fell on Zach's back. *Hello, sailor.*

"Crap!" He shot to his feet, steadying himself against the wall.

Where the hell am I? This can't be happening!

The room looked skiffy. A hotel, based on the lack of personal items. Dark and dirty, the way he felt. Dust motes swirled in front of a lone window. A breeze flapped the moth-eaten curtains. Outside, the music of congested traffic played. Beeping horns, shouts, testosterone revved engines. A morning rush-hour symphony.

1

He didn't want to look at the man again, not by a long shot. But he couldn't help himself. He inched the sheet down to the corpse's waist despite the trembling in his fingers. Two red circles punctured the man's belly. Bullet holes. Dark blood stained the sheet.

Gah! I slept in it! But I'm not gay!

Zach's stomach swelled. His ab muscles tightened. Bile lit his throat on fire. He clamped a hand over his mouth.

Where the hell's the john?

Across the room, light seeped out below a door. His stomach kicked as he stormed the bathroom. Whatever he had for dinner last night decorated the floor. Nachos, maybe.

But I don't eat nachos.

The thought of the junk food bucked his gut again. His foot skated through the mess, tossing him forward. He caught the sink, locked his arms around it and thoroughly finished his business. Above the mirror, a light bulb hissed, sizzling like bacon.

Quit thinking about bacon!

Another round emptied his stomach. Dry heaves rattled him, tying his taut abs into knots. He looked at his reflection, not a pretty sight. Bloodshot eyes. Sweat matted bed hair. Even his usually carefully maintained five o'clock shadow appeared unkempt, little stubbles of dirt.

What happened last night? Think, Zach, think!

His sludge-filled, lazy brain wouldn't cooperate. The commercial jingle for his favorite teeth-whitening product wormed through his thoughts over and over and… *EZ Brite makes your teeth clean, EZ Brite gets out the green…*

No! Focus…last thing I remember was killing it at the dance club…

Something rang a bell in his head, a giant cathedral gong of a bell. It quieted fast, nothing more than a dim memory of a dream.

He sat on the toilet, his legs shaking. His head throbbed, on par with the worst hangover in history. But he hadn't overindulged in years. Wouldn't do it, his body a temple and all that stuff.

How did I get here? And I'm not gay!

2

Too weak to get up, he reached over, swung open the bathroom door. Looked at the dead guy across the room. Still in bed. Still dead. And still really, really naked.

Crap.

Okay, call the cops. Wait. They'll think I did it. But I didn't…did I? That's crazy. I'm not a killer. I'm a male dancer! Damn good one, too.

Deep breaths. Easy does it. Be cool.

On seafaring legs, he climbed off the toilet and stumbled toward the bed. He averted his eyes, darting his head around the room like a frightened gazelle. Anything to avoid looking at the guy and his horrible, accusing eyes. And his three belly buttons.

Maybe he's not dead.

Zach crept toward the bed, praying for a sign of life.

"Hey…look, guy, you okay?"

He stuck a shaking hand over the corpse's face, fingers splayed. Then he changed his mind, nudged him with his elbow instead. Seemed less gross.

"Mister? Hey…wake up."

Nope. Still dead as disco.

Dammit! This doesn't happen to me! This can't happen to me!

A cool breeze burst in from the open window, goosing his exposed butt cheeks.

Pants! Where're my pants?

Zach gave the room a quick once-over. Nothing. No sign of his clothes. Or the dead man's either. He dropped to his knees, his cheek to the floor. Too dark to see under the bed. He reached in, swept his arm.

Tiny legs skittered across his hand. "Ah!" He yanked back, flapping his hand. Nothing under the bed except for critters. Bad enough he had to touch a dead guy.

No pants. No phone, no wallet, no anything.

Think!

EZ Brite, nice and easy, seconds to apply, really breezy…

Stop it!

Okay. Stuck in a room, who knows where, with a dead guy. And no clothes. And I know I'm not gay.

3

Then he saw the shoes, couldn't believe he'd missed them earlier. On the dresser next to the dead guy. Not very stylish, boxy old-man shoes. But they'd have to do.

With an eye on the dead man, he quickly snatched the shoes away. No need pissing him off now. Somewhere he'd heard vengeful ghosts don't like to have their property stolen.

Now I'm just being stupid. Tend to the matter at hand, worry about gay ghosts with a mad-on later.

The shoes devoured his feet, way too big. In the bathroom, he padded the extra space with toilet paper. Not a bad makeshift cure. On the way out, he glanced at himself in the mirror. Come to think of it, he didn't look all that bad. He struck a pose, arms in front, muscles tensed. One for the ladies.

I still got it. Even when I feel like crap.

A quick wink at his reflection and he left the bathroom. Wearing only his banana hammock and old-guy shoes. All he had except for his wits.

First…where am I?

He pulled the billowing curtain aside. The familiar skyline of downtown Kansas City greeted him, a horizon of buildings. An old-fashioned fire escape ran down the side of the building, the metal stairs rusted into a sunset orange. Clearly an old hotel on the outskirts of downtown.

Bang, bam, bang!

The pounding on the door shoved his heart into his throat. He jolted upright, straight into the window frame. *Crack.* Pain seared across the back of his head. Small lightning bugs danced before him, then cleared the room. Like he had to do.

Bang, bang, bam!

"Open up. KCMO police."

I can't get busted! Someone with my looks will never last a day in prison!

Zach didn't even think about it. He climbed out the window on autopilot.

Clang!

The fire escape shook, rattling like an oncoming locomotive. Behind him, fists pounded on the door and voices shouted.

4

"Open the door *now!*"

Zach raced down the stairs, pivoted at a landing to the next flight. His shoes clopped, the heels lifting and dropping, his toes straining to keep them on. Three flights down, two to go. A Riverdance of footsteps poured into the room upstairs. Panicked voices. A woman screaming.

He slowed on the last flight and tiptoed. Maybe they wouldn't hear him. Or look out the window. Once he hit the alley, the sound of a squawking police radio drifted down, urgently static.

Zach stumbled down the alley, the shoes slowing his progress. He lifted his legs high, shuffling the shoes in a ridiculous parade march. Sunlight illuminated a street ahead, a beacon to freedom.

Then what? I can't run through the downtown streets in my thong.

Next to a dumpster, he stopped. He only had minutes, if that. Time enough for a quick dumpster dive for something to wear.

Runch, spak. The dumpster lid hit the brick wall, way too loud. Zach clenched his teeth, looked behind him.

"*Hey!* What're you *doin'?*"

Zach froze. He couldn't see the source of the voice. Maybe the dead guy's ghost already haunted him.

"Leave my stuff alone!"

No, not a ghost. A woman's voice. With his hand still on the lid, Zach peered behind the dumpster. A woman lay beneath cardboard boxes, a grocery cart full of clothing and junk next to her. Using the wall as a crutch, she climbed to her feet. A gloved finger jabbed out.

"What're you doin' in my dumpster?"

"Ah, sorry, ma'am." Zach strapped on his million-dollar smile. "Didn't know this was your turf. But, as you can see by my wardrobe…" He flourished his hands over his torso. "…I'm kinda in a bad way. Just wonderin' if I could borrow something to wear?"

"Hah!" She squinted, a distaff Popeye look. Or maybe she only had one eye, Zach couldn't tell for sure since she never released the squint. "You ain't homeless. Homeless boys don't got muscles like that!"

"Shh! Please keep your voice down. Can you help me out? Please?"

Fsk, fsk, fsk. She rubbed her chin, her whiskers rivaling Zach's five o'clock shadow. "How much it worth to you, sonny boy?"

"What? Look…I don't have any money on me…"

"Then whaddaya got to offer?"

Crap. I don't have time to bargain. "I…uh…can dance for you. Maybe?"

She doubled over, screaming. Going into a seizure, Zach thought. When she straightened, though, tears of laughter moistened her good, open eye. "What kinda dumb-ass you take me for? A dance? What're you some kind of pervert or somethin'?"

"No, ma'am. I'm…a male dancer." Zach eyed her cart, planning his move. Surely she wouldn't miss one item of clothing. Add it to his quickly growing list of crimes.

"A stripper?"

"No…a male dancer. We prefer to be called—" It'd take too long to explain the important difference to a grocery cart lady.

Taking a cue from the bag lady, Zach squinted and pointed down the alley. "Hey, what's that?"

"What? Where?" When the woman turned, Zach snatched the top piece of clothing and dashed toward the street.

"Hey! Dammit! Stop!" The woman's already impressive vocal chords hit a new high. Her screams bounced off the brick walls, a chorus of bag ladies. "I been robbed! Help! Thief!"

Zach didn't slow. He unfolded his stolen treasure as he ran. A short fur coat, clearly faux. He thrust an arm into one sleeve, swung it over his shoulders, and hooked his other arm through it. It provided little coverage, leaving his midriff and thong exposed. Better than nothing. His arms pumped as he hopped over discarded syringes and broken glass. One shoe finally gave out, staying behind. Near the end of the alley, he hopped on one leg. Behind him, footfalls clanged down the fire escape. A volley of voices lifted, shouting.

"Stop!"

Zach barreled into the street, skidding to a halt on the sidewalk. Blocks away, a siren screamed. Red and blue cherries spun in the distance, coming his way. Business men and women stopped to gawp at him. A woman dropped her cell phone and gasped. For once, Zach really didn't enjoy an audience.

"Just go about your stuff, ladies and gentlemen." Placating hands went up. Zach put on a serious yet gentle face, one meant to say, *I'm harmless. Please ignore me.* Sorta hard to do when you're standing downtown in a sexy golden thong, a fur coat and one shoe.

A car horn blared. The cop car stuck in rush-hour traffic. Footfalls crunched over broken glass in the alley at his back. Coming his way.

Nowhere to hide. Can't blend in.

A cab! Across the street. Suddenly self-conscious, Zach clamped his hands over his butt cheeks and scurried through the traffic. Tires screeched beside him. *Chang!* Bumper met bumper. One driver hauled out of his dented car and ran toward the other driver, busy screaming and punching at the sky.

Yeah! Get your mad on, guys! Give the crowd something to look at besides me!

Zach slid into the taxi's backseat.

Behind the steering wheel, the cabbie was contemplating a breakfast burrito. Zach sunk down low. "Hi. Can you take me to Overland Park?" The only place he could go. The only person who could help him, the person who always helped him.

The cabbie peered into his mirror and dropped the burrito. He gave Zach a long look before pronouncing judgment.

"A little early for Halloween, boss."

Zach looked ridiculous, no doubt about it. He really, really hoped no one had their phones out, shooting his posterior for posterity. "Long story and a bad morning."

Zach peeked over the back of the seat. Several cops milled about the fender bender, pointing fingers and issuing orders. The bag lady joined the fracas, hassling one of the cops. One policeman tilted his hat back and stared at Zach through the windshield with "lock him up and throw away the keys" eyes. Zach yelped and flattened on the seat.

"Cops lookin' for you, kid?"

"No! What makes you think that?" Zach's desperate laugh sounded like a chicken's hiccup.

"Let's just go, 'kay?"

The cabbie sighed. "Don't look to me like you got any cash on you." He took a bite out of his burrito. Crumbs flaked away, dotting his beard.

"I'll give you anything. Whatever you want! Just get me outta here. I swear I didn't do anything illegal! How 'bout…I let you in free for a month at my club?"

"Oh? You own a club?"

"Well, no…I perform there."

"Wait…you a stripper, for God's sake?"

Again with the nasty labels and prejudice. Male dancers continually fought an uphill battle. Still, no time to fight, just retreat. "Whatever, yeah."

"Why in hell I wanna go to a male strip club? I ain't gay."

"Neither am I! Wait…you got a wife? I'll give her free passes!"

The cabbie chortled, burped, and wiped his mouth. "You think I want her lookin' at you guys? No way. Sorry." He slammed up his meter flag. "Out."

"Okay, okay, fine. You take me to my sister's in OP and she'll pay you double."

Like the window in an old cash register, the driver's eyes lit up, practically dinging. "For real?"

"Yeah, my word's solid, brah. Just…get me out of here! Now!"

"Deal. Better not be welching on me."

"I'm not…please, can we go? Fast?"

"Fast is my middle name." He chunked the gear in drive, flipped the flag down. Lurched into the street, leaving a small token of rubber behind.

Zach stayed low and held his breath. They waited for an eternity at a stoplight. Zach poked his head up and risked another look back. The cops had their hands full with the jammed up traffic. And the dead guy in the hotel room.

The car leaped forward, along with Zach's stomach. Probably the only way the cabbie knew how to drive. Zach closed his eyes, trying to find his inner core. With his ringing head and his frazzled half thoughts, no amount of meditation helped. Instead, he found the EZ Brite jingle again. Or, rather, it found him. His damn new mantra. He loosened the beast, singing under his breath.

"…makes your smile white and purty, open wide and bring on the flirty—"

"Hey! You singin' that EZ Brite song?"

"Um…yeah."

"I *love* that song!"

Chapter Two

Zora stared into the dryer, stuck in the deep knee bend of advanced pregnancy. Unable to get up. Of course that's when the doorbell rang, the way it always seems to happen. Her knees wobbled, unsteady, threatening to dump her over. In her condition, she felt less than athletic.

"I'll get it," screamed Nikki, her six-year-old. Always ready to open the door to strangers, but can't open and shut a clothes dryer. Maybe if Zora installed a TV above it.

By the time Zora rolled onto her side and negotiated the six-point maneuver necessary to get to her knees, the real screaming started.

Nikki. Justin caterwauled alongside her.

Eight months pregnant or not, Zora bounced to her feet.

Hold on, kids! Mom's coming to the rescue!

She looked hurriedly around for the closest potential weapon and grabbed a bottle of stain remover. *Hey! Any old port in a storm!* Bottle in hand, she hustled down the hallway.

Nikki stood in the open doorway, still yelling at the top of her lungs. Her hands were fastened over her four-year-old brother's eyes, not so much his screaming mouth. Zora took one look over her daughter's head and joined the line-up, her hands slapping down over Nikki's eyes. *Figures.* Zora's brother Zach stood outside wearing nothing but a fur coat, a golden thong and a stupid, shameless grin.

"What in the…what now, Zach?" She turned her linked entourage away, shushing them.

"Oh my God, Zora, you've gotta help me! I've had the worst day! My wallet and phone and pants are missing, and I'm not gay, and I woke up next to a dead guy, and I just spent forty-five minutes singing the EZ Brite song with a cab driver, and he can't sing at *all*, and—"

"Wait, wait, wait." Like a traffic cop, Zora stuck her hand up. Zach could never tell a story for his life. Or keep it together in a crisis. Something she'd come to expect from him over the years. "Back up a minute. What's this about a dead guy? No…wait…" She bent over, lightning ripping up and down her spine. "Kids, it's just Uncle Zach. I need to talk grown-up stuff. Go do your homework."

"It's summer, Mommy!"

"Well go play, watch TV, torture the neighbor…whatever you do all day."

They scampered off at a dangerous inside sprint, singing the EZ Brite song. "*EZ Brite* takes out the *greeennn…*"

"Get in here, Zach! Before the neighbors see you!" Still holding the stain remover, she wagged him in. Then thumped him in the head with the bottle.

"*Owwww*, dammit! Why'd you *do* that?"

"Because I know you and I know this isn't gonna be good."

"Come on, sis." His grin blossomed into a face-wide smile, one that never worked on her. "I didn't do anything. Really."

"Yeah, right."

He jacked a thumb behind him. "Um, I sorta told my cab driver you'd pay him. Please? Cash only, Bennie doesn't like plastic. You know I'm good for it."

Good for nothing, more like. With a sigh, she grabbed her purse.

After the transaction ended, she stormed back inside. Mad as hell. Even worse, her brother was sitting on the sofa with her nice pillow covering his junk. Watching TV.

"One hundred twenty bucks! I had to pay him double, Zach!"

He shrugged. "I'll pay you back."

The purse flew, missing her brother by a mile. Still felt good.

She sat far away from Zach. Pretty much for his safety. If she could reach him, she'd kill him. "*What* have you done this time? Why are you showing up at my house in your stripper bikini, freaking out my kids and—"

"Whoa, whoa…I'm a male dancer. An entertainer. I've told you—"

"Save it! What's this about a dead guy?" She couldn't believe he was somehow involved with a dead person. Well, strike that. Yes, she could. Her brother's screwing up and her constantly bailing him out formed the backbone of their relationship. Sorta a take-take relationship. Nothing surprised her anymore when it came to Zach. "Tell me from the start. Try and be coherent for a change."

"Okay." He held his hands up, struggling for mental balance, she supposed. *Good luck.* "I woke up this morning…didn't know where I was. And I felt hung-over."

"So, you tied one on?"

"No! That's just it, Zora…you know me. I gave up drinking after high school. Pretty much."

"Yeah…pretty much. Go on."

"Anyway, I was in some dumpy hotel room. Downtown. And…there was a dead guy in bed with me. Naked!" For the first time, he showed something resembling fear. His eyes grew round, glistening. "But I'm *not* gay! You *know* I'm not! Not that I got a problem with that, you know. Some of my best dancer pals are gay. But it's gonna look—"

"Let me see if I have this straight. You woke up next to a dead man. And you're worried what sexual orientation people might consider you?"

"Well…yeah. *Duh.*"

This time his sheepish smile pushed the wrong button. A pillow flew across the room. *Flumph.* Contact. "Hey! Cut it out!" Immediately, his fingers flew to his hair, primping and patting it back into place.

"Duh yourself, idiot. And don't 'duh' me! You've got a much bigger issue here! The police are gonna be looking for you! Why didn't you *call* them? So *stupid!*"

"I'm not stupid," he muttered.

"What you did is stupid, no other word for it! Things could've been straightened out! You coulda got off the hook. But *noooo!* Instead, you hightail it over here, dragging me into… *whatever!*"

"Zor, I'm sorry. Really. But I had no choice. I couldn't remember anything. *Nothing*. I know I'm not a killer. I know I didn't do it. I just don't know how it happened. Or what happened, really." The boy she remembered growing up with, her protector, surfaced. No play-acting, no put-on fake charm that only works with ditzy women. Then he blew it. "And…I can't have anyone thinking I'm gay."

Her eyes rolled, straining as much as her lower back. "You sure the guy was dead?"

"Yep. Touched him and everything."

"Great. DNA, genius!" She tapped her lip, thinking. When she used to work, she'd come across similar cases. Without the dead body, of course. "Maybe he died of natural causes…you know, from pleasure?" Her turn to smile. She couldn't help it. Mean, maybe, but it's not like he didn't deserve a little dig.

"*What?* No! I told you…I would never…"

"I can't believe this. Just can't believe it…surely you remember something."

"Nothing."

"Before you woke up…what's the last thing you recall?"

He closed his eyes, thinking hard. A Herculean task. As if being channeled by a smarter spirit, he spoke slowly. "I was dancing at the club. Killing 'em. Um…not, you know, like what happened to the guy I found. But…I remember…I found a note stuck into my speedo along with some mad cash. Something about…" His eyes rolled open. A snap of his fingers followed, a few synapses sparking. "A woman! She wanted to buy me a drink at the bar!"

"Okay…it's a start. Did you meet her?"

"I think so."

"You *think* so?"

"Yeah. Look, everything's…hazy. Like a dream." He gasped. "You don't think…you don't think someone roofied me or something?"

"Kinda looking that way. If what you're telling me's the truth. I swear to God, Zach, if you're lying to me, I'll—"

"No, Zor, no." He shook his head slowly and stood to display his melodramatic hurt and humility. That wasn't the only thing on display.

"Oh, for God's sake! Cover back up. Gah. I've got kids in the house!"

"Hm? Oh, crap, sorry." He scooped up the pillow, buried himself beneath it. "But I'd never lie to you. Not you. Never. Anyone but you."

She believed it. Even if his admission as to lying to everyone else pretty much deflated his humble moment. "Whatever. So…you met the woman for a drink. You get a name? Phone number?"

"If I did, it wasn't on me when I woke up."

"Well, you remember the woman, right? What'd she look like?"

His slow-burning Cheshire cat smile forecast his juvenile lust. Sometimes men really suck. "Yes! I'm remembering something…" He pulled cupped hands back and forth to his chest. "She had *huge*…um, sorry…"

"Great. Just what I didn't want to know. Like I want to know *any* of this. Anything else you remember about her?"

"Sorry. The mind's run dry." He tapped his temple. Zora swore she heard a hollow echo somewhere. "And I'm hungry. Got anything to eat?"

If she had another pillow she would've hurled it. "Oh, sure, you want me to cook for you? Maybe a full meal? Some nice protein to build your muscles up?" She ignored his happy nod. "Idiot! You're on the run for murder and you wanna eat?"

As sure as a piano crushing down on her brother, she saw the weight of his dilemma finally sink in. He crashed into the sofa. Cradled the pillow over his face, hugging it tight. A terrified little boy. Of course she was going to help him.

"Guess not."

"Alright, alright, let me think…you had a drink at the bar?"

"I…think so."

"So…the bartender. Let's go talk to him."

His eyes, his demeanor brightened. "You'll go with me?"

"I'm not gonna lend you my car. Last time I did that, Phillip was pissed for a week. You still owe us for the scratch."

"Oh, yeah…that." Dreamily, he smiled up at the ceiling, a nostalgic recollection. Zora didn't even want to know. He pulled out of it, faster than usual. All business again. "Seriously, Zor...I think someone's framing me. Out to trash my good name and reputation."

She couldn't help another eye-roll, sort of an involuntary reflex with Zach. "First of all, and as usual, the world does not revolve around you! You really think someone would go to all the trouble of framing you? Maybe it's about the dead guy. And not you."

"You mean...like I was used...or something..." His voice trailed away, the thought incomprehensible, even though Zora knew he spent a better part of his time catting around and using women. Karma can be a bitch.

"Maybe. Suck it up, tough guy. And as far as your good name and reputation? Hah! When did *that* happen?"

"Hey, I've got a good reputation in the male dancing field."

"Stripper field."

"Male entertainment dancer."

She dropped it. Bigger fish to fry. "Let's see what the bartender has to say. We'll go from there."

For once, Zach sat quietly, his eyes big and blinking at the TV.

"Zach? You okay, big brother?" When she looked at the TV, a fist enclosed around her stomach. Either that or the damn baby was kicking up a storm.

"Turn it up, turn it up!" Zach picked up the remote and flicked the volume louder. "Shh, quiet..."

"...late breaking news from Channel 8, Senator Hal Turlington found dead in a downtown Kansas City hotel room today at the age of sixty-two. Official cause of death has not been released. There are reports of local police inquiring about a man of interest..."

"Crap...I'm the man of interest, aren't I, Zor?"

"Oh, damn, damn, damn! You couldn't just wake up to a *normal* dead, naked guy! *Noooo*, you had to wake up next to a damn dead senator! Oh, damn..." If Zora could've jumped out of her chair, she would've. Instead she fork-lifted herself out, then paced the room. "Dammit! What're we gonna do now? You're involved in killing a senator!"

"I didn't kill him!"

"The police don't know that! And now they're gonna be looking for you!"

"How? There wasn't anyone who could identify me. I don't think."

"Again with the 'you don't think'! That's your problem, you never think!"

"Do too!"

"And now...now the cops are gonna be searching everywhere for you! Dragging me and the kids and Phillip into this whole damn mess!"

"Well...Phillip doesn't need to—"

"Gah. Quiet! I gotta think about this...it doesn't look good for you, Zach!"

"I know..."

"Do you? Well, you better get used to it! And now you've made it ten times worse by running!"

"I have to clear my name! Or I'm going down, sis! They can't connect me with it, I'm telling—"

"How do you *know* this? For all you know, you checked into the hotel under your own name!"

"Doubt I'd do that."

"Charming! And what about your DNA you left everywhere?" She wrinkled her nose. "Maybe even in the sheets!"

"Now that I *know* I didn't do—"

"Shut up!"

"Sis, I have a clean record. Even if they find my fingerprints, they don't have—"

"Clean record, clean record...let me see...clean record...Oh! Guess you forgot about your high school drunk driving bust?"

Enlightenment smacked him upside the head. "Wait...oh yeah, crap. Well, they, whaddaya call it, expectorated it from my record."

"Gah! 'Expunged'! And just because they did that, they still have your fingerprints on file!"

"I'm in big trouble, aren't I?"

Zora didn't deem his ludicrous question worthy of an answer. She continued pacing, back and forth, burning a path into the carpet. Stewing.

Zach stood. The pillow fell. Oblivious to his near naked state, his usual way of dealing with life. He sucked in a deep breath, buried his face in his hands. Building up to a dramatic moment, always onstage. "Look, Zora, I'm sorry I brought you into this. I'll understand if you can't help me. I'll just leave. Again...I'm sorry."

"Would you go get some of Phillip's clothes to put on, for God's sake?"

"But...Phillip's like four sizes bigger than me!"

"Cry me a river! Just do it, dammit!" Before she could stop herself, she rushed across the room. Her arms went around her brother's back, possibly a little too violently. She closed the distance for a hug, as close as his semi-nudity and her protruding stomach would allow. "Dammit," she said. "Of *course* I'll help you. You're my brother."

Cries from upstairs broke the moment. Zora pushed away. "Great. All I need. My *fourth* child waking from his nap."

As she hurried from the room, she heard her brother struggling through his limited mathematical abilities. "Wait...Zor...you only have *three* kids."

With a diaper bag strapped over her shoulder, Zora hustled Nikki and Justin out the front door. "Come on, kids. We're going on an adventure."

"Adventure," parroted Justin.

Nikki, already the sullen teen before her time, whined, "Mom, what're we doing? I'm busy!"

"Girl, I don't wanna hear about busy. Just get in the back seat. Enjoy the sunshine. Remember what that is?"

"So stupid!"

"Zach," she yelled up the stairs, "Samantha's already in her seat by the door. Grab her on the way out." A task surely even he couldn't mess up. Then again, when it came to her brother, all bets were off.

Justin struggled with his seat, always a battle. No wonder her swear jar had evolved into a bucket. "Just stay still...almost....there." *Clack.*

"Mom, really, what're we doing? Why was Uncle Zach naked?"

"He wasn't naked, Nikki. Just underdressed."

"Is he in trouble again?"

"No." *Yes.* "We're just gonna try and help him with some stuff."

Zora pressed down on the pedal, revving the engine. Hoping to speed her brother along, never the quickest guy to get things done. She checked her phone, fully charged and 10:30 a.m. Plenty of time to clear her brother of murder, get back and have dinner on the table for Phillip by six.

Despite the situation, Zora laughed when her brother stumbled out of the house. He had Samantha's carrier seat in one hand and kept his pants cinched up with the other. A belt lapped off the end-loop, a wagging brown tail. The suit looked like a relic from the'80s, entirely too large and probably never in style.

As Zach rolled open the back door of the minivan, he sighed. "I know, right? I look ridiculous. Doesn't Phillip own any regular clothes? Jeans, a polo, anything?"

"Hey, stylin' guy, shut up and get in. It's better than you waving your…golden sack around town."

"Golden sack, golden sack, Uncle Zach has a golden sack!" Justin joined his sister in song. "Golden sack, gold—"

"Kids, enough! I don't wanna hear that again about your uncle!"

"But, Mom, you said it first!"

"Again. *Not* a democracy." She turned in her seat, double-checking Zach's strapping in of Samantha. Unbelievably, a grin threatened to eat his face off. Clearly proud of the song his niece and nephew had concocted in his golden sack's honor. No shame. "Get in, Zach."

He climbed in beside her, fidgeting with the suit collar. "Still don't know why I have to wear the jacket and everything."

"Look, if they're onto you, they won't be expecting you in those clothes, right?" Kinda lame logic, but she just wanted to shut up his grousing. In all honesty, Phillip didn't have any "fun" clothes. Something she'd been working on for years. Accountants aren't the most fashion-conscious people.

"I guess."

Zora punched in the strip club address to her phone, turned the speaker on. "Okay, I've been thinking. Say you have been set up." As

18

she backed down the driveway, she made sure little ears weren't tuned in. For once their attention devouring electronic gadgets served a useful function. "Or it may be about the senator. But we have to consider both options."

"'S'what I've been sayin'."

"Yeah, fine. Do you have any enemies? I mean as far as..." Finger quotes. "...'male dancing' is concerned? And I'm not talking about broken-hearted women."

"What kinda cad you take me for, Zor? I don't break—"

"Zzzzzz. Huh? Sorry, you put me to sleep for a minute. The truth. Enemies?"

He stuck an "aha" finger up. "Well...there's Fireman Freddie!"

"Keep your voice low," she sang. "Dare I ask who—or what—Fireman Freddie is?"

"Oh, he's just this guy at the club. He's jealous of me. I guess we sorta have a rivalry. I mean, his shtick is he dresses up as a fireman. So been there, done that. No artistry whatsoever."

"Oh, the shame. How is this relevant?"

"He used to make fun of my gig. 'The Banana Hammock Bandit.' Always laughing at me, saying things behind my back—"

"And then he went out with the head cheerleader and wrote nasty stuff on my locker and tattled on me to teacher. Whatever. How about leaving high school behind for the time being? Get to the pertinent point."

"I had a custom-made...um..." Zach snuck a look behind him, lifted an eyebrow. "...thong, painted up like a banana. Green and yellow and totally awesome! Even put a couple dark spots on it like it was ripening. Threw down a lotta bank on it, too. My jam!" He rocked a fist up. Zora didn't feel like rocking along. "Anyway...Freddie said it looked like dirty underwear..."

"Hah! Gross. I can't believe you paraded around in that! What were you thinking?"

"Oh, whatever! At least it was original. Anyway...we've been fighting since, trying to one-up each other, dogging the other."

"So corporate skullduggery in the male dancing trade?"

"Yeah, something like that. Recently Evans—he's the manager— gave me the top spot. Demoted Freddie to opening act. Didn't sit well with him." He snapped his fingers, twisted in his chair. The suit didn't turn with him. "As a matter of fact, he threatened me after that."

"Whoa. You mighta led with that. What'd he say?"

Zach put on political airs, thrust up a power thumb. Lowered his voice. "Something like, 'I know you're the greatest dancer here, Zach— '"

"Ahem!"

"What? So, he said, 'You're better than I am, Zach, but I'll take you down.'"

"Yeah…did he really say that?"

"Pretty sure."

"I'll just pretend that's what he said. Anyway, we've got two leads now. The bartender and Firecracker Freddie."

"Fireman Freddie."

"Like I care."

What she did care about was the sign in the parking lot of Zach's "work" place. *The Bone-In Beef Club* stood tall and proud on a pole, probably like most of the strippers at work. A cheesy blinking drawing of a filled thong supplied the logo, a particularly large bulb acting as an unnecessary exclamation point in the middle. Zora regretted not bringing blindfolds.

"Mommy…what's Bone-In…Beef…" Before Justin could struggle through the rest of it, she cut him off.

"A steakhouse, honey. Uncle Zach's a waiter here."

"But I thought he was a ballet dancer!"

She hissed out irritation, shot Zach a look that could kill.

Chapter Three

Zach strutted past the doorman and gave him a courtesy nod.

"What's up, Zach? Looking sharp." He said it with a chuckle, however, like he didn't really mean it. Muttering something to himself, the doorman returned to counting the wad of currency in his hand.

Zach certainly didn't feel sharp in the square, oversized suit. But it's the man who makes the clothes, not the other way around. Act confident, look confident, be confident. Easier said than done when you're on the run.

Onstage, Brian was torturing the pole with his flabby thighs. He stomped around to the power chords of a cheesy arena rock anthem displaying the grace of a wrestler. Just one look and Zach could detect at least ten pounds of extra body weight hugging Brian's midsection. Two slumming women ignored his desperate attempts at sexy, gabbing over their cocktails. Brian never made it beyond matinee performances, no small wonder. He gave male dancers a bad name.

Zach spotted Alan behind the bar, polishing a glass. Shirtless as always. Which kinda made Zach wonder if the bartender's hairy chest might be a health code violation of some sort.

He slid onto a barstool. When Alan finally looked up, he gave Zach a double-take.

"Dude! Surprised you're up and around already!"

"Alan. Whaddaya mean?"

Alan stretched across the bar and lowered his voice. "Man, last night you were out of it. I mean, totally wasted."

"Yeah...here's the deal, Alan...you ever know me to get hammered? I mean, really?"

"Dunno. Guess not."

"Thing is I don't remember what happened. Help a brother out?"

"You don't remember anything?"

"Nothing. I remember doing a killer set. Some chick slipped me a note. Wanted to buy me a drink. That's it."

"Oh yeah...her." Alan grinned, nodded his head as if privy to a secret.

"What about her?"

"Dude! You don't remember her?"

"No."

"Hot, dude. I mean as long as you're into plastics. Like fo' realz. You sat at the stool next to where you're sitting now."

Zach's gaze wandered over to Brian. Clomping around like a baby learning to walk. Shaking his belly, hypnotic waves of fat rolling and rolling and rolling...

Then he remembered...

As soon as Zach saw her sitting there, he knew she was the one who'd slipped him the note.

Hotness flocks to hotness. Her legs practically travelled up to her waist. A llama's length of neck rose from her form-fitting midnight-blue dress. Bulging cheekbones narrowed her eyes to slits.

When she smiled, nothing shifted, just a twitch of the lips. And her breasts were abnormally big.

Clearly she'd had some work done. Which suited Zach just fine. People should take pride in their appearance.

With one leg crossed over the other, a high-heeled foot tapped out her boredom. Waiting for him.

She's not gonna be bored much longer. The Banana Hammock Bandit is in the hizzy-house!

Still in his banana hammock (club policy), he slipped onto the stool next to her. By now, he knew to expect the cold leather of the stool on his butt cheeks, so he locked his smile with clenched teeth.

"Hey there." His voice squeaked a hair once the first bite of cold landed.

"Hey there yourself." Not shy in the least, her gaze wandered over Zach's body before connecting with his eyes. His kind of woman.

"So, I'm Zach. The Banana Hammock Bandit."

"Yes, I know." She tipped her drink back, grinning around the rim of the glass.

"What's your name?"

"Cat."

A fitting name. "Well, Cat, pleasure to meet you." He shook her hand. Dry as rope with wrinkles that didn't match the rest of her enhanced presentation. His first clue she might be a cougar, making "Cat" even more fitting.

"Likewise. What'll you be drinking?"

"What're you having?"

"Scotch on the rocks."

"Um…too many calories for me." He smacked his abs, loving the solid sound that resulted. "Gotta keep in shape, you know."

"Of course."

Alan, appearing bored as usual, meandered over. Why management didn't make him wax his chest blew Zach's mind. "What'll it be, Zach?"

"White wine, cut the way I like it."

Never approving of Zach's preference, Alan rolled his eyes but did as he was told. Half wine, half water. Special treatment for the star attraction, of course.

"So, Cat…you like my act?"

"Very much so."

"Yeah? Tell me…what'd you like about it?" Hearing from Zach's fans was one of his great pleasures. He listened to all criticism, naturally, had a rhino skin. But he especially liked the compliments. Because they were always right.

"You know what I like."

23

Well, no, not really.

But he could venture a pretty educated guess. His night was about to get interesting. Before he could lean over and seal the deal with a quick kiss, Alan blocked him with his drink.

"White wine…kiddy style."

Zach ignored him. Jealous, plain and simple. "Why don't you tell me what you like, Cat?"

He smiled, hit the dimple spot. One he practiced often in front of the mirror. Now it'd practically become a natural reflex.

Her fingers played across his bare (and freshly waxed, thank you very much) chest. "I like your moves. Show me more." She slipped a twenty dollar bill into his G-string, let her finger linger a bit.

Club policy insisted on as many lap dances as one could shake out in a night. Zach put his money-maker to work. He jumped off the stool, trailing his fingers over her knee. Teasing her, leaving her with a special memory. On one leg, he twisted, slapped his thighs. Bent over. Slowly, slowly, until his head looked between his spread legs at her. Upside-down, her smile looked like a frown but he was used to it. Part of the male dancer's intensive training. He straightened, his back still to her. Now for the big finish, one of his specialties. The butt shake. He poked his butt cheeks out, gave them a nice balletic swirl. Then he tensed his hips, his upper thigh muscles. Small tremors moved through his midsection. Working their way toward his cheeks with the intensity of an earthquake. *Bang!* Full-on booty shaking, fast as hummingbird wings.

He swiveled, bowed to her clapping. Always a gentleman. He reclaimed his throne next to his queen for the night.

"I want you to come with me. Tonight."

That's all he needed to hear. To celebrate his victory, he slugged back the wine, downing most of it. Bubbles tickled his nose, a first. Alan probably gave him champagne for a laugh, knowing how many calories were in it. Didn't matter, though. His victorious mood couldn't be dampened.

A smattering of belated applause met his impromptu performance.

Only one person mattered though. "I think that sounds like a killer idea, Cat."

"You have no idea, Zach."

"I'm finished here for the night. Let me just go back and grab my clothes."

"I'll be waiting for you out front. We'll take my car."

Even better. The gas gauge read nearly empty on Zach's Celica.

Before he left, he dropped a hand on her knee. Walked his fingers down her leg. Always leave 'em wanting more.

But as he entered the dressing room, the room turned dark, even darker than usual…

———————————

Zach gasped, snapped to attention. Before he turned to stone, he averted his eyes from Brian's undulating belly.

"I remember," he said. "Or at least, I remember the woman and the drink."

"Good for you," said Alan. "You wanna gold star or what?"

"What happened next? All I remember is going to the dressing room. Then…I dunno what I did!"

"You passed out's what you did. Evans wasn't too happy 'bout it either. Wanted you outta the club fast. Bad for business."

"But I wasn't drunk! I only had one glass of wine."

"Yeah…I know…watered down."

"You didn't give me anything else, right?"

"Hell, no! I'm a professional." He scratched a hairy nipple. *Sktch, sktch, sktch…*

"The woman…she musta' roofied me."

"Really, Zach? *Really?*"

"Yeah, for realz. I mean, nothing else explains it. So I left?"

He shrugged. "Guess so. I saw Fireman Freddie helping you outta the dressing room. He took you outside. Then hit the stage five minutes later."

"I knew it! Freddie had something to do with it."

"Hey…he's a fireman after all. Helping people any way he can." Alan laughed at his joke.

Zach, on the other hand, was less than amused. "Okay. This woman. You got any paper on her? Credit card name? Debit card?"

"Nah. Thought it was a little weird, too. I mean, who pays with cash anymore?"

Dammit.

—————————

"Okay, so I got proof I was roofied." Zach slammed the minivan door behind him.

"Mommy, what's roofied?"

"Hush, Nikki. What kinda proof?"

"Well, I was watching Burly Brian roll his flab all around the dance floor and then I remembered—"

"Burly Brian, Burly Brian, Burly—"

"Quiet, Justin! Can you tell the story without, um, any details about your work, Zach?"

A tough chore, but Zach managed. Quite well, too, he thought.

"Hardly proof, Zach," said his sister.

"But…I don't drink to excess! You know that! I had one drink!"

"Still nothing. You really think that's gonna win the day in court? 'I didn't perform this heinous crime because a woman I don't know slipped me a mickey'? I don't think so."

"You think I'm going to court?"

Zora sighed, stuck the gear into drive. "Let's go see Fireman Freddie."

"Who are these people, Mom?" asked Nikki. "Fireman Freddie and Burly Brian and—"

"Don't you worry your pretty little head about it. They're just work-friends of your Uncle Zach's."

"Waiters?"

"Um…yes."

"Then I wanna eat at the Bone-In Beef—"

"No, you don't! And don't tell Daddy that, either."

Zach turned, gave his niece a wink. Arms folded, Nikki slumped back against the seat and snorted. Clearly puzzled by the mature world of adults.

Freddie lived on what Zach's parents used to call "the wrong side of town." Further proof Zach was the more accomplished male dancer. A utilitarian rectangle, bricks and curtain covered windows were the apartment complex's only design elements. A junkyard's worth of heaps and broken down autos clogged up the parking lot. Kids played on the sun-scorched lawn, sticks and cans their toys of choice.

Zach thought if Freddie took the trade more seriously, he might be able to upgrade his living quarters some day. But he wasn't there yet.

Based on the shape of the door, someone had been looking for Freddie pretty badly. A couple of holes sat at the bottom, a kicking calling card. Didn't surprise Zach one bit. Freddie didn't make friends easily.

Metal music blared out from inside the apartment. Zach pounded hard, rattling the other doors in the hallway.

Once Freddie opened the door, his smile fell.

Busted.

"What the hell you doin' here, Caulfield?" Still working out his high school failures, Freddie never once referred to Zach by his first name.

Zach gave as good as he got. "I think you know, Filmore."

Freddie whipped a towel from around his neck, twisted it. Snapped it in front of Zach. More high school stuff, locker room bullying. "Dunno what you're talkin' 'bout."

"I think you do. Look...I just wanna' know what happened last night. That's all."

"What happened? You got shit-faced's what happened. Now get outta here! You're interrupting my workout." He grinned, a little dark gap between his two front teeth. Zach always thought he should call himself "Lisping Freddie." He'd let him know it a couple times.

"I didn't get shit-faced. And you know it."

"Facts don't lie, Caulfield."

"What facts? Dammit, Filmore, just tell me what happened!"

"Don't think so." Freddie started to close the door.

Zach stuck his shoe, well, Phillip's shoe, inside. Always worked in the movies. The door crunched hard, Phillip's shoe providing little protection. Pain shot up through his body, reigniting his hangover styled headache.

"Ow! Goddammit! I can't believe you did that!"

With his shoulder into it, Zach smacked the door back. Shocked, Freddie stumbled, his arms wagging to the side for balance. He caught himself, growled. And charged Zach, arms outstretched. He dove, snagging Zach around the waist. Zach fell back into the door, slamming it shut.

"Get off me, dammit! Stop—"

"No way, a-hole! You started it!"

The stench of Freddie's sweat filled Zach's nose. Clammy hands gripped Zach's arms and swung him around. Still dizzy from the night before, Zach's stomach flip-flopped. The floor rocketed up to greet him. On the way down, his head banged into a workout bench.

"Agh!"

Freddie dropped and straddled Zach. Pulled a fist back.

Zach's hands flew up to his face. "Not my face, Filmore, don't hit me in the face!"

Freddie's unibrow dropped. He studied his fist, shrugged, then punched Zach in the gut.

"*Ooof!*" Zach fought back, carefully adhering to his own rule. Fair was fair, after all, and even though Freddie was about the ugliest dancer he knew, no one deserved to have one of their money-makers decommissioned. He let fly a flurry of slaps to his nemesis's arms, chest, stomach.

Smek, spak, pop, takketa, tak...

Freddie slapped back. Fingers struck palms, a furious game of patty-cake.

Zach knew he had the disadvantage. Just this once. His roofie hangover. But his legs were stronger. He wrapped them around Freddie's torso, his ankles crossing at his back. And rolled. The motion

28

dizzied Zach. He thought he might hurl on his opponent. But their positions reversed, Zach now on top.

"Who's the tough guy now, Filmore?" Zach unleashed his fury, his anger, his fear. In a flying slap fest of pain. "You had enough?"

"No!"

An open palm caught Zach's cheek. "Dammit, we had an agreement!" He slapped back, branding Freddie's cheek a bright shade of red.

Things turned ugly. A double slap, forward and backward across Zach's cheek. Zach clawed back, rolling his open hands like a boxer. Fingernails bit into skin. Zach squealed, scared of the damage to his cheek.

Zach had to end it. Tomorrow night he was due to perform. No one would pay to see the Beat-up Banana Hammock Bandit. He clenched his hands together and brought them down onto Freddie's chest. The air left Freddie with a *whoosh*. Reflexively, his legs bounced up and dropped with a *clomp clomp*.

"'Kay. Think I've had enough now, Caulfield."

So had Zach, not that he'd ever admit it. Out of breath, he rolled off. The two dancers lay next to one another, their heads beneath the weight bench.

"Knew you couldn't take me."

"Whatever, Caulfield, you sucker slapped me."

As much as Zach wanted to truly show him who the stronger dancer was, other issues needed to be prioritized. And his sister and her kids were waiting out in the minivan.

Rain check, though. Oh, yeah, it's so on.

"Okay, Filmore. Let's start over. I won the fight—"

"Did not. Not fairly!"

"Um, yeah, I did. Anyway. Not important right now. I wanna know what happened last night. What you did to me."

"Man, I didn't do jack to you. What're you talkin' about?"

"Were you workin' with the hot blonde from last night?"

"What? That plastic babe? No! Hell, no!"

Zach leaned up on his elbows, raised a fist. Slowly opened his fingers, one by one, to expose his palm. "You want more of this?"

"No, Jesus, just…stop! All right! I ran into the broad when she was leaving. She stopped me, asked me if I'd like to make a hundred bucks. I thought, hellz yeah, a private party!" Zach shook his head. Another disgrace to the dancing community. They were artists, after all, not prostitutes. "But instead she just hands me the Benjamin, tells me to grab your clothes and crap and help you out to her car."

"You never met her before? Saw her before?"

"No. Damn…I think you bruised my side."

"I'll do more than that if you're not telling me the truth."

"Why'n hell I be lying?"

"Just sayin'."

"What's this all about anyway? I mean, you come crashin' into my place, yellin' and slappin' me like a bitch and—"

"*You* slap like a bitch."

"—actin' all urgent and shit. What's goin' on? What're you into?"

"Nothing. Or maybe big trouble. I dunno. It's what I'm tryin' to find out. What kind of car was it?"

"I dunno. Huge gas guzzler. Black Caddy, I think. Yeah. And she had a driver. Big guy. Helped you into the back seat. I just figured you were gettin' your party on, man."

"Yeah, some party. She roofied me."

Freddie let out a low, long whistle, finally impressed by the serious nature of Zach's plight. Even though enemies, Freddie also understood the professionalism of keeping one's body in shape. "Dayum, man, that's rough."

"Tell me about it."

"So…what happened next?"

"No idea. Thought you might know."

"You know everything I do."

"Hey…you said she told you to get my crap. What about my wallet and my phone? My clothes?"

"Tossed that in the back with you. I know 'cause I snagged a tenner from your wallet. You owed me from a couple years ago."

"I paid that back!"

"Bullshit you did. Anyway, like I tole you, I tossed your crap in on your passed out ass and the car took off, nearly burning tread on my shoes."

"You happen to get the license plate?"

"Whadda I look like? 5-0? I'm a fireman!"

"Yeah, not a very good one, either." Fully recovered, Zach kipped up on his feet. Maybe not so fully recovered after all. Freddie'd left a few sore reminders. A nemesis not to be underestimated. Just undervalued.

"Better than your lame act, Caulfield." Copying Zach's move, Freddie kipped up, too. Chests out, they stood glaring at one another. Nostrils flared. The tips of Freddie's mustache flew up with each heated breath. Seriously invading Zach's personal space.

"We'll continue this another time, Filmore. Once I get my problems worked out."

"Count on it. Maybe a dance-off, the audience judges."

"I'll be there with my G-string on."

Zach turned at the waist, clasped his hands together and flexed in a side chest mode. Freddie curled over, his tensed arms shaking. Zach relaxed, nudged Freddie's shoulder as he made for the door. Maybe he still had a little high school left in him, too.

At the door, he turned. "Freddie?"

"Yeah?"

"You know...I'm not gay, right, man?"

The question took Freddie by surprise. He popped out a gasp, his eyes wide beneath his beetle of a brow. "Yeah, shit, of course. Except for that suit, man. Kinda gay."

Zach nodded, left more determined than ever to prove his heterosexuality to the world.

Chapter Four

Her brother's disheveled appearance didn't worry Zora. Her husband's ripped suit kinda bugged, though.

"What the hell?"

"Mommy!"

"Shit, sorry." She let her kids play out their put-upon grief before she attacked Zach. "What happened? What'd you do to Phillip's suit?" She flicked the torn jacket pocket. A cash register *ka-chinged* in her head. "You're paying for this, Zach."

"You know I'm good for it."

"Right. Heard that before. So...what? Did you and your little buddy decide to wrestle over who's the better dancer?"

"Kinda."

"Gah. Men. So stupid. What'd you find out?"

"Not much. The mystery woman paid off Freddie to take me to her car. That's all I got."

"Make? License?"

"Believe me, I asked. I'm not stupid, you know."

Some things are better off left unsaid. But Zach had plenty to say about his clearly embellished story of heroism. "...and that's how I crushed the Fireman!"

"So...we're at a dead end."

"Looks that way."

Zora closed her eyes. Trying to separate the reality of her restless kids from the fantasy of Zach's play world. Hard to do with two of her kids arguing in the back seat. And her brother humming a damn commercial jingle next to her.

"Zora?"

"What? I'm thinking!"

"Well, yeah, thanks and all that…but is Samantha, you know your ten-month-old—"

"I know who she is, Zach!"

"Is she okay? I mean, she hasn't made a sound since we left."

"Oh, for God's sake. You an expert on parenting?" She turned around, sighed. "Kids, is Samantha fine?"

Nikki, well-trained at something, leaned over her little sister. She gooed and gahed at Samantha while rummaging inside the baby seat. "Everything's fine, Mom!"

Zora raised her eyebrows, stared at Zach. "She's my golden child. Nice. Quiet. But once she starts talking and walking, the trouble starts again. But right now? She's wonderfully quiet! Like I wish others would be in the car! Can I get back to thinking about your mess?"

"Yep, just a concerned uncle." Before she could retreat back to her quiet, contemplative place, Zach started humming the EZ Brite jingle again. An unwelcome soundtrack to her thought process…

What am I missing? What would I have done back in the business?

Zora cursed silently. Her swear bucket change was running low and she couldn't afford to curse out loud.

Think, woman! What would I do if I was still working security?

Still sitting in Fireman Freddie's apartment lot, she killed the engine and plucked out her phone.

"Here." She handed it to Zach. "You've got GPS on your phone, right?"

"Yeah."

"Pull it up, log in with your password."

"You know, I was just thinking about that."

"Don't strain yourself too hard."

Zach tapped out the numbers, handed the phone back. "All logged in."

Zora found the right app, did a little finger work. Her heart stuttered when she read the location of Zach's phone.

"Um, Zach?"

"Yeah?"

"The address here is 1636 Swankler Lane, right?"

"Yeah. Why?"

"Because your phone's here. Same address."

"Son of a...um, dog! Freddie lied to me. Had it all along. Alright, I'm going back in, round two."

Before he opened the door, she grabbed her brother's arm. "Hold up a minute. You believe Freddie about not having your phone?"

"Yeah, guess so. Guy's kinda' a tool, but, yeah, whatever."

"And he confessed to making $110 off your trauma. If he's dumb enough to fess up to that, why wouldn't he go all the way? I mean, about having your phone? Why lie?"

"Unless he's still working for the woman!"

"Or...just be cool a minute, Zach." Zora looked over the parking lot.

Junkers, works in progress, cars patched together by rust and dust...

A song from one of her kid's shows burrowed into her head: *One of these things is not like the other...*

Several cars over, a Hybrid was backed into a parking spot. Smoke plumed from the exhaust. Strips of sunlight struck the top of the car and the interior. A perfect spotlight picked out a bald dome. Hunkered down in the car.

"I think I found your phone."

"What? Where?" Zach hitched up his butt to peer beneath.

"Don't look now. But a guy down in the lot. Sitting in a Hybrid."

"Whaddaya talkin' about? We're being followed?"

"Ixnay on the ollowfay!" Zora gave him crazy urgent eyes and nudged her head toward the back seat.

"Who's following us, Mommy? Beary Brian?"

"Quiet, honey. No one's following us."

"Um, I'll go have a word with the guy, sis."

"No you don't. I've seen how you have words with people. Ahem!" She tapped Phillip's wasted jacket pocket. "Let me handle this."

"You're kidding, right?"

Immediately, she put him in his place with her special, narrow-eyed look. A skill she'd mastered years ago, the shorthand of siblings. "*Not* kidding."

"But…Zor, you're like, what, eight months pregnant!"

One, two, three, four… "So help me, Zach. I'm trying to be patient here. And I'm trying to help you outta your latest cluster. But, by God, you're trying me. Before Phillip started sticking his…ah…babies in me, you remember what I used to do, right?"

"Yes." Properly chastised, Zach tucked his hands between his legs, folding like a losing poker hand.

"So. You're gonna tell me how to handle this?"

"No."

"Da… *darn* skippy! Now, make yourself useful and watch the kids."

She shut the car door behind her, leaving her brother sputtering something inconsequential.

No time for nonsense. Phillip expected dinner at six.

The building Freddie resided in ran the length of eight top and bottom apartments. Two entrances at opposite ends. Conveniently, the Hybrid was parked between the doors. Zora kept her head low, walked into the entrance Zach had come out of. She'd no idea if their shadow knew her by sight, how long he'd been following them. But past experience taught her surprise could be a valuable weapon. Certainly the Hybrid's driver wouldn't expect her to approach him. She walked down the hallway, placed a hand on the opposite exit. Took a deep breath.

Truthfully, she felt great. Except for the living watermelon in her body, of course. But it'd been a long time since she'd experienced the rush of the job, the thrill coursing through her veins. Been a while since she'd felt anything in her body except for babies. After this, she planned a serious talk with Phillip. About going back to work and his impending vasectomy. The one she'd just decided he was going to have.

Like a technologically obsessed child, something she knew a little bit about, the man dedicated his full attention to the phone in his hands. With both windows rolled down, an easy target. *Amateur.*

Her heart pounded. The baby pressed down on her spine, inducing some serious back pain. Probably best to sit through the interrogation.

At the passenger side, she leaned down.

"Excuse me, sir. I wonder if you could help me out."

He jolted. An unhealthy wheeze escaped him. Like a busted teen trying to hide his porn stash, he flailed with the phone before slipping it into his sports jacket pocket. A greasy smile slid over his initial shock. Greasy and extremely phony. "Why sure, little lady. What seems to be the problem?"

She yanked open the door, slid inside. She kept her purse handy in her lap. Never leave home without it. "I locked myself out of my apartment. Could I borrow your phone to call the super? I hate when they don't live on the premises."

His tongue crawled over his lips, chasing a chuckle. An inappropriately smug and condescending chuckle. "Now that does sound like a problem, missy. Mighty big problem." Tautly drawn buttons barely kept his formidable belly, one to give Zora some serious competition, in check. He patted his stomach trophy. "Always glad to help out a damsel in distress."

"Thank you."

He wiggled his head, kept laughing. She'd been made, no doubt about it. Playing with her.

"Lemme just grab my phone outta the glove box." With a grunt, he leaned over, his shirt sleeve traveling high over gorilla-hairy arms.

"I don't think so." She grabbed his wrist and slammed his hand against the glove box. Gave it a little twist.

"Dammit, lady, what're you doin'? Leggo!"

"Not 'til we have a little chat. So…apparently you know who I am. Who're you? My mother always taught me not to talk to strangers." He didn't answer. She grabbed two of his fingers, yanked back on them. A great way to break the ice.

"Let go, let go, let go! Christ almighty! Alright, alright…Mrs. LeFevre, alright!"

She released him. He flapped his hand before him, working the pain out.

"Ready to talk?"

"Wasn't any need to do that to my hand!" He licked at his fingers, making a sloppy dog at a bowl sound.

"Oh, really? Then let's see what you have in your glove box?" *Clunk.* The lid fell down, exposing a pistol. A 6 mm, kinda femme, but more than enough to do some damage. "This how you're gonna help a lady in distress? Oh, and don't call me 'little lady.'" She snagged the gun, held it out of his reach.

"Alright, let's just cut the game-play, little…ah, Mrs. LeFevre. Yep, I know who you are. Overland Park housewife, mother of three. Whoops, soon to be four. I also know you're not the type to use a gun. So…" Another sickly Santa smile, his lips as red as his ruddy cheeks. "Why don't you just hand it over to me before someone gets hurt?"

Sexist. His mistake. "Oh, really? If you'd truly done your homework, you'd know what I used to do."

"Ah…"

"Just as I thought. Dolt. I was in the security field, did some detective work. A consultant for one of the biggest firms in the country. Denham and True. Heard of 'em?"

"Um, yeah." Suddenly his girth deflated. Not by much, but a difference that made Zora's day.

"So, then, you know I'll use this gun. In fact, since you pretty much insulted me, I may as well pop one in your kneecap. How's that sound?" She closed an eye, stuck her tongue out, Annie Oakley style.

"No, no! God, no! Stop!" His shriek rose higher than a frightened pig's squeal. Made her baby kick, a certain satisfaction. He shut his eyes, hands sheltering his knee. "What do you want?"

"That's better. Let's start over." She heightened her voice, batted her eyes, imitating the stupid girls she despised in college. "Hi! I'm Zora. Zora LeFevre! Swell to meet you! I'm an Aries and I *lovvve* boy bands! What's your name?"

"Martin. Bob Martin. Private Investigator."

"How exciting!" She dropped the giddy girl act. "Tell me, Bob, what's going on with my brother?"

"What? I don't know any—"

"Have it your way." Stay-at-home parenting really sapped Zora's patience. Particularly today. She raised the gun again, almost hoping she could pull the trigger. "Kiss your kneecap goodbye."

"Okay, okay, okay!" Jazz hands fluttered. "Just…put it down. I was hired this morning to find your brother and follow him. And just let my employer know what he's up to."

"Why?"

"I dunno. Really, I don't! I'm just a P.I. Sometimes it's best if I don't know too much."

"Real professional."

"Hey, lady, sometimes it takes being a professional to stay alive."

Don't I know it?

"Fine, let's try a different tack. Who's your boss?"

Puckered lips switched side to side. A deep breath sucked in, blowing out his belly. Jazz hands lowered. And, man, did Zora hate his smile.

"Well, now, what's it worth to you?"

"What's it worth to you? One or two knee caps?"

"Tough talk only gets you only so far, missy. Here's the deal…let's just say I'm good at taking insurance out on myself. My employer sent me a telephone, a burner, early this morning. The only way I'm supposed to contact them. Everything's conducted through anonymous calls, texts and drop-boxes. I really don't know my employer's name. But I'm sure someone like you could suss my employer's name out with the burner phone. Thing is it's stashed away somewhere safe. You want it? You're gonna have to pay for it."

"Still might be fun to blast your knees." A bluff. She needed the information. And Martin knew it. Easy to tell by his new-found confidence.

"Doubt you're gonna do that. 'Cause I'm assumin' by your desperation your little brother's in a heap of trouble. You need my information to bail him out."

"How do I know you're not lying to me? Just to save your precious knees?"

He laughed. Zora was killing 'em today. "'Cause contrary to what you believe, I'm a professional. Looks like this job's already gone ball's up…um, excuse my French…" Zora sighed, shook her head. She'd heard worse from her four-year-old. "So, I need to make a little cash outta the deal. Get paid for my time. You're my new employer."

"Yeah, some professional. So much for dedication to your previous employer."

"It is what it is, lady."

Crap. She didn't have time for this. Tonight's lamb chops hadn't even been thawed out yet. If dealing with the creep could end this mess sooner, so be it. Zora'd learned long ago, sometimes you gotta deal with a little extortion. "What's your price?"

His lips clicked, an eyelid closed. Human calculator. "How 'bout…$10,000?"

"Yeah, right. How about two grand?"

"Sold."

Zora brayed. Couldn't be helped. "Really? Just like that? Hell, I was prepared to offer up $5,000! You really are an amateur!"

"No, wait! $5,000, then!"

"Too late, done deal. Sucker!"

"Dammit!"

A muscular arm snaked in, grabbed Martin by the neck. The detective's face bashed into the horn, tapping out a few notes.

"Let him go, Zach!"

Zach stood outside the window, still playing horn taps with Martin's face. "Hey, I heard a scream, thought you needed help, sis!"

"You mean like in rescuing?" Her daily quota of sexism had already gone way over limit. "That was him screeching, dumb-ass. Everything's under control! Gah. Honestly, you men. Even eight months pregnant, I could take down both of you sexist pigs."

"Sure, sis."

"And you left the kids in the car by themselves?"

"Hey, I locked the door and Nikki said she could watch—"

"They're not dogs! And Nikki's six years old!"

"But that's the age I started babysitting you."

"Irrelevant!" She raised her voice to be heard over the horn. "Let him up already!"

"Oh. Yeah. Sorry." Tenderly, Zach leaned Martin back into his seat. Straightened the detective's thinning hair with a few hand pats. "Sorry about that, mister. Just thought my sister was in—"

"I'm bleeding!" Martin wiped his nose, pulled away a red splotch. Stared at it disbelievingly like he had a stigmata.

"You'll live. Now before my brother rudely interrupted...first things, first. The phone?" She held her hand out, palm up.

"What phone?"

"Martin, I don't know if you're playing dumb or are just dumb. I saw you with a phone. And I know you have my brother's phone. Hand it over."

He groused while digging into his jacket pocket. "Fine." He tumped it into her hand, not a happy camper.

"Thank you. I'll get the money for you. We'll meet back here in an hour. Deal?"

"Wait...what money?"

"Quiet, Zach! The grown-ups are talking. Sound good, Martin?"

Snurf. "Sounds good."

"Oh. Since you consider yourself somewhat of an insurance expert, I'll just hold onto your little gun as a little bit of insurance of my own." She waggled it about. The heft of it felt good, the grip conforming nicely to her hand.

"Now, wait a minute, lil...Mrs. LeFevre, that ain't part of the deal!" Martin reached for the pistol. Zach latched onto his wrist, pulled it back.

"Too bad. Business can be cutthroat. See you in an hour. Ta-ta for now." Zora wanted to make a bad-ass exit, one to rival her entrance, she really did. But once the thrill was gone, the baby made its presence known. Strongly. Took her three tries to lift out of the car. But damned if she was about to ask for the big, bad male contingent's help. "Let's go, Zach."

"What's going on, sis? I don't know about your bringing that gun. They kinda freak me out."

"Just come on, already. We haven't got much time. I'll fill you in on the way to the bank."

"Whatever you say." Zach sprang away from the detective's car in a ridiculous slow-mo jog, hands jotting up and down. Something he probably learned from all those episodes of Baywatch he rotted his teen brain on. Then he ran back. Leaned down into Martin's window.

"Um, dude, sorry I bloodied your nose and all. Do you have my pants by any chance?"

"Your pants? What in hell?" Old school style, Martin started cranking his window up by the handle.

Zach clumped a hand down on the window's edge. "They're really good pants, dude. Tear-away specials I had made. Really want 'em back."

"No, I don't have your damn pants! Get off my car!"

"Sorry, mister. But, really, you gotta do something about your weight. Not only is it a disgrace to your body, but you're a walking heart attack. If I were you, I'd turn that mass into muscle. Yeah!" He poked Martin's belly. Martin stared back in disbelief, cranky. Zora didn't blame him, not really. "Just watch your sugars, breads, carbs...start working out and—"

"Come on, Zach!"

———————

"Your pants, Zach? Honestly!"

"I like my pants. They're great pants." Zach hitched up the excess baggage on Phillip's pant leg and sighed over his lost love. "Awesome pants."

"Forget your damn pants for a minute!"

"Mommy!"

Her kids had been so abnormally quiet, Zora'd almost forgotten they were along for the ride.

Eavesdropping, little detectives in the making. "Sorry, Justin. Mommy won't cuss again." *Yeah, right.* "I'm just a little stressed out right now."

She wheeled the minivan into the bank's drive-thru lane. "I mean it, Zach. Phillip's gonna hit the ceiling when he notices the money gone. You've got to pay it back this time."

"Hey, no prob, sis. My word's as good as gold."

"Uncle Zach's got a gold sack, Uncle—"

"Stop it *now*, Justin!"

Zach and Justin exchanged a smirk, the kind usually reserved for playgrounds. Exactly where Zora felt like she was playing on.

"Just pay it back."

"So…this detective's gonna give up the name of his employer for two grand?"

"More or less."

Zach kicked his feet up on the dash. "Then we're done. Thanks, sis. I knew you'd come through."

"Hardly done. I've learned not to bet on long-shots. And get your feet off the dash!"

Clump.

Zora drove onto Shawnee Mission Parkway, maneuvering between the cars zipping in and out of the lanes, everyone in a frantic hurry. Business as usual. But one car in particular didn't seem so usual, one that caught her eye. Three car-lengths back. Carefully staying that distance. A black Caddy.

She adjusted the mirror, quietly said, "I think we've got company."

"What?" Zach straightened up, looked behind him.

"Mom, what company's coming over? Not that boring guy from Dad's work again, I hope. Anybody but him."

"Quiet, Nikki. Zach, your fireman buddy said your mystery woman had a black Cadillac, right?"

"Yeah."

"I think they've been tailing us since the bank."

"Why'd I ever get out of bed this morning?" Zach drew a hand down his scraggly cheek, nestling into a woe-is-me state-of-mind.

"Really, Zach? Would you rather be back in bed with your buddy?"

"Good point."

"Okay, just hold on tight. Everyone strapped in?"

"Yes, Mom…I'm *not* a baby."

At a stoplight, Zora looked back. Tinted windows hid the Caddy's driver. Sunlight gleamed off the car's freshly washed exterior. She revved the engine. Looked left, then right. No cops. One final car zooming through a yellow light on the cross street.

She floored the gas pedal. The minivan's tires screeched, then propelled the van through the light. Behind her, a horn blared.

"Mom, you ran a red light!"

"Whoops. Sorry, kids."

Zora cut the wheel right, pulling in front of a Town Car, missing it by inches. The driver saluted her with a choice finger.

"Mommy, he gave you the finger!"

"Shame on him!"

One arm over the seat, Zach watched their pursuer. "He's catching up!"

"Who, Mommy? What's happening?"

"Part of the adventure, Justin." The Caddy kicked out of stealth mode. Speeding up now, closing the gap. Yep, definitely following them. Not a good thing.

"Come on, Zora, step on it! This is, like, the slowest car chase I've ever been in."

"Like you've been in a lotta car chases, Zach. Shut up. Let me drive."

Zach turned a white shade of fear. "Zora…what if he catches us? Go faster!"

"I've got my kids in the car. I'm not gonna go all speedway." With a speed limit of 45 mph, she was already pushing it at 55.

The Caddy whipped right, bypassing the cars in the other lanes. Catching up fast, throwing caution to the wind. Serious business on his mind.

"Crappity, crap, crap!" Zora needed an edge, some way to shake him. *How?*

"Mom, is that guy chasing us?" Nikki, staring out the back window, ran her words together. Showing signs of life for the first time today.

Justin shrieked. Scared or excited, Zora couldn't tell. Weird kid at times.

"Nothing to worry about, kids. Mom's got it under control."

The speedometer inched up to 60…65. Be bad if a cop pulled them over. Worse, though, if their mysterious pursuer caught them. Not on her watch, not with her kids on board.

"Hang on, kids! Just like your videogames. Fun!"

Justin continued his one-note shriek, not so much in fun mode.

Zora leaned into it, cranked the steering wheel. The minivan charged back into the left lane. Passed one car, then another. Ahead of her, a yellow van poked along in her lane, almost at a standstill. Behind them, the Caddy drew closer, its grill shining, full of silver teeth. Zora wrenched the steering wheel hard.

Krink.

She nicked the van's bumper. Lost control of the wheel. Panicking, Zora over-corrected, sending the minivan thrashing across two lanes. They lurched right, Nikki tumbling into Justin, finally cutting his screaming off.

"Mommy, get her off me!"

"Kinda busy, Justin!"

Zora wrangled the van into one lane. Punched it. Not far behind them, the Caddy passed the yellow van, the driver now laying on his horn. Staying glued to Zora. She floored the pedal, leaving everyone else far behind. Except for the damn Caddy. 70, 75…80…

Down the road, a stoplight flicked to yellow, then red. Cars crossed through the intersection. Her timing had to be spot-on. She twisted the wheel, dropping them back into the far left lane. The Caddy mirrored her.

"*Arragghhh!*"

"Mom, Justin just puked!"

"Terrific!"

The stoplight swam up. Still red. And still lots of cars passing through the intersection. Nearer and nearer…

300 feet to the light, 200 feet… The cross traffic didn't slow. Neither did Zora.

"Everyone, hang on! One more bit of fun!" *I hope.*

A Volkswagen entered the intersection ahead of her, a final straggler. Taking a turtle's sweet time. On-target for a t-boning.

"Slow down, Mom! The light's red!"

"Crap, Zora!" Zach thrust white-knuckled hands against the dash, digging in for impact.

100 feet from the intersection…

Move, you slow-ass Volkswagen!

Zora roared into the intersection. She cranked the wheel, one hard tug. The VW's driver finally sped up, barely bypassing her swinging tail-end. Then Zora slammed on the brakes.

Rrrrrrrrrrr….shzzzzzz…

The minivan spun, a half loop. Rubber marked their trail. The two right wheels lifted off the ground, clopped back down.

"Whoa!" Zach's head banged into the ceiling. Nikki screamed. The van fishtailed. The steering wheel took on a life of its own, spinning left, then spinning right. Zora grabbed the wheel, taming it. They shimmied, then shot off down the intersecting road like a rocket.

The Caddy driver was less fortunate. As was the VW. In her mirror, Zora watched the Caddy fail to make the turn. It spun out, its back end slamming into the side of the Bug. Smoke signals of distress went up from the Volkswagen's engine.

Slowing down to 70, Zora barreled over a dip in the road. Up they went, then down, a hellish rollercoaster. Zach grunted, his teeth audibly snapping down. Zora gripped the steering wheel tight, her hands shaking. *Steady, nice and steady…*

Another check of the mirror. No sign of the Caddy. No pursuing cops.

60…55…a nice snail's pace of 45…

Zora let out a long breath, hadn't realized she'd been holding it.

"Everyone okay?"

"Mom, I'm scared! And Justin's all gross!"

"You okay, Justin?"

"Yeah…"

"Samantha! How's she, Nikki?"

"She slept through it all, Mom! What're we *doing*?"

Good question. Things were getting dangerous. She couldn't take her kids with her any longer. But what to do with them? The answer seemed clear, one she didn't like.

"Well, kids…we've got one more stop to make…then I guess you're going to see your grandparents."

"Yay!"

Zach stared at her, white as bone and eyes big as golf balls. Then he pitched forward, heaving onto Phillip's shoes.

Dammit.

"Uncle Zach blew chunks, Uncle Zach blew chunks, Uncle…"

On the way back to Fireman Freddie's place, Zora rolled all the windows down. Smelled like a boy's locker room inside the van. And the kids let Zora know about it, too, time and time again. Getting rid of them for the day was sounding more enticing by the minute.

"Hush, kids, I'm not real happy about the smell either." She glared at her brother.

"Sorry, sis." He avoided looking her in the eye. He knew better. "Hey…" His voice raspy, he cleared his throat, spoke up. "We're, like, twenty minutes late. You think Martin will still be there?"

"Yeah. Guy like him won't walk away from two grand."

When Zora pulled into Freddie's lot, the neighborhood kids were no longer playing outside, but everything else remained the same. Martin's Hybrid sat in the same spot, the engine still idling. No sense in breaking with tradition, Zora reclaimed her earlier parking spot.

"Wait here. Don't do anything stupid. Try not to get sick again." She said that to her brother, not her kids.

Cash envelope in hand, gun in purse, she waddled toward the Hybrid.

Martin was dozing behind the wheel, his double-chins planted on his chest.

"Wake up, Sleeping Beauty. Your Prince Charming has arrived."

Martin didn't move. In fact, he didn't snore, either, something Zora had no doubt he excelled at.

"Martin?"

Nothing.

Wary, she reached inside the open window. Shook his shoulder. Slowly he tipped, fell onto the console. Blood spattered the shirt barely containing his belly.

Oh, dammit. Damn, damn, damn…

Gut-shot.

Stay cool, girl. Think.

Carefully, she grabbed his wrist. Felt for a pulse. Nada. Deader than Elvis.

Call the cops or not to, that is the question…

Under any other circumstance, she would. Would have in the past, damn straight. But this would be doubly as bad for her brother. Possibly even her. And she couldn't clear Zach if implicated in a double murder.

Plus, she had her kids in the van, had to get them to safety. First priority.

Other than getting Phillip his damn dinner on time tonight. She probably needed to call him…

The phone! Martin's employer's phone!

The last thing Zora wanted to do was pat Martin down, dead or alive. Plus there was the whole issue of contaminating a crime scene. Leaving her DNA behind. Of course her DNA was already all over the car from her previous visit. As was Zach's.

Hell with it.

She tapped Martin's jacket pockets first, his favorite phone hidey-hole. Nothing. Grimacing, she dug hands into his pants pockets, avoiding the blood as best she could. A tin of chewing tobacco, lint, change. Trying to roll him over to get to his rear pockets took the wind out of her sails. Especially with baby on board. Martin's body wobbled back and forth as she pushed. Finally the heft of his belly took over, dragging him to the floorboard. A lot of work, no payoff. Empty back pockets. She scurried around to the passenger side, checked the glove box, the floor, the back seat. Fast-food wrappers and empty cigarette packages, Martin's memorial.

Not good.

Apparently, Martin never even left the parking lot. If he had, he'd have the phone with him. Money meant everything to a guy like him.

Unless, of course, the killer snatched the phone. Which made sense, too. A scary kind of sense. Scary because the killer had been brazen enough to kill Martin in broad daylight, possibly in front of a yard full of kids.

Definitely have to get my kids to safety. Even if I dread taking them to my parents as much as being locked up. Well, not quite. But almost.

"How'd it go, sis?"

Unlike her brother, she'd learned how to perfect a poker face. "Could've been better."

Zach lowered his voice. "What happened?"

"Remember how we were worried about being late?" Zach nodded. "Well...we can now refer to the detective as the late Bob Martin." Casually, she swung around to see if little ears were listening. Fully enamored with their handheld electronics.

"Oh...man...oh, man..."

"Open the door this time, Zach. Lean out. Don't get any on the car."

Chapter Five

Zach couldn't believe it. Another dead body. Not his day. And things were about to get worse. Visiting his parents.

"So, what happened to Martin, sis? I mean, I know what happened to him. Duh. But what do you really think hap—"

"Little ears, Zach!" Zora tugged on her ear, a reminder. "We'll talk about it after we drop the kids off."

Zach examined his phone, anything to take his mind off their impending parental showdown.

"You happen to make any phone calls during your, ah…outing last night, Zach?"

"I'm checking…nope, but apparently I recorded something. Hang on…I'll play it on speaker phone…"

A rustling sound, similar to airplane turbulence. Voices, only Zach's identifiable. Although damn slurred. *So embarrassing.* And a woman's voice in the background, hushed but whiskey deep. Sexy in a way. Fit the woman from what he could remember of her.

"… *yur the hottest thang since jaleeponies…heh, no wait…jalopies…no…yur so hot, you could melt—*"

"Oh for God's sake, Zach, turn off the speaker!"

"What? Why? Might be a clue here."

"Turn it off and give it to me!" Zora released a hand from the steering wheel, held it out to him. With the speaker off, she cupped it to her ear.

"Mommy, no phone while you drive!"

"I know, Justin, but this is a special exception. Now, hush."

Zach scooted over, shoulder to shoulder with his sister, and listened. More come-on lines, apparently to the mysterious Cat. Even drugged, at the top of his game. Something banged. *Footsteps?* A key jangled. A door opened and shut.

"… *come on feel th' noiseee! Girrrlzzz rock yur boysssss…*" Zach smiled, pumped a fist. Roofied or not, he could still kill his dancing anthem.

Zora sighed, held the phone away from her ear while Zach started the song over again.

"What?"

"You're singing some stupid rock song. Repeatedly!"

"Yeah! That's my jam! My song!"

"Zach, you *can't* sing. Um…I'm almost afraid to ask, but…were you dancing for your abductor?"

He scratched his head, closed his eyes. Searching the dusty attic of his muddled mind. A memory unfolded and swirled into focus…

"… *feel the noiseeeeeee!* Yeah, baby! Thash…what I'm talkin'…'bout…"

Zach ended big, the only way he knew how, and tore off his pants. Embellished it with a pelvic thrust. "Bam!"

Sitting cross-legged on the edge of the bed, Cat caught his pants. Smiled. "Very nice."

"Hey…nice is my…whaddaya call it? Middle name." Zach checked his phone. Wanted to make sure he recorded his performance.

"What're you doing, Zach?"

"Recordin' my killer moves…"

"Now we can't have that."

In seconds, the large chauffer crossed the room and yanked the phone from Zach's hands.

Shut it off. And pocketed it.

"Hey! Thash my phone!"

"You'll get it back later," said Cat.

Stumbling back, Zach banged into the wall. *Dizzy.*

"Maybe you better lie down, honey." Cat patted the mattress.

Zach ran, dove onto the bed. "Got more things than…sleep on my mind."

"I'm sure you do."

Something didn't feel right, though. Zach looked around, couldn't remember how he got there. A dark, kinda crummy hotel room. He had Cat pegged as a sugar-momma, thought she'd go for more upscale digs. Not the hotel of infinite despair.

But, really…how'd I get here?

The last thing he remembered was dropping in the Bone-In's dressing room.

What's wrong with me?

Cat stroked his chest, let her hand linger. "Looks to me like you're not up to much of anything, tiger."

"Cat and tiger, Cat and tiger…" Struck him as funny. He giggled, his head riding a merry-go-round. "I'm alwaysh up for…fun."

But for once he didn't feel like it. And the big guy across the room seriously gave him the creeps.

"Whatever you say."

"It'sh what I shay." He sat up, trying to anchor the room down. "Whoa."

"Just lie down and take a little nap. Plenty of time to play later." It hadn't escaped Zach's attention that Cat had remained dressed, not exactly up for play herself. As he reached for her, the silver-haired giant in the corner jolted, took a step forward. Giving him serious, steely "kill you" eyes.

"Wanna…play, Cat…but does Lurch have to…watch?"

The big guy sneered. Maybe even growled a little. Hard to tell with cartoon mice squeaking in his head.

"What do you want me to do, ma'am?" At nearly seven feet tall, the guy was tightly wound, ready to split the seams of his chauffer's suit. Or maybe he wanted to split Zach open, the way he glared at him.

"Right now, we just wait, Dennis. Remember the plan."

"Dennish?" said Zach. "No…wait…really? *Dennish?*" Clearly European, with an accent thick as his neck, the chauffer didn't look like a Dennis. Maybe a Boris or something James Bondish like that. "You're killin' me here! *Dennish?*"

Dennis looked less than amused.

"Cat...I think yer hawt...way hawt. But I'mma not...I'm not into...kinky crap. Can Dennish pleash leave?"

Before Cat answered, someone knocked on the door.

"Ah...that's our final guest. Right on time."

"Hey...hey...no orgiesh..."

"Be quiet, Zach. It'll all be over soon." She stood, fluffed her hair. Primping. "Get ready, Dennis."

Silently, Dennis moved beside the door, his back against the wall. Cat opened the door. Two old men stood in the hallway. Maybe just one old guy but he wouldn't stand still, shaking and shimmering like a paint-mixing machine.

Their voices rose, a heated argument.

But to Zach, it sounded like "rar, rar, blar, rar, dammit!"

Dennis stepped out of the shadows. Grabbed the old guy, lifting him off his feet.

Cat smiled, a canary-eating grin.

Things just got weird. "Hey...hey..." Zach swung a leg over the bed. When he stood, his legs turned into rubber, snapping him back into bed. "Whash goin'...on?"

Dennis raised a fist, brought it down. Jabbed a hypodermic needle into the old man's neck.

"Shtop...I mean, strop...hey..."

The old man went limp in Dennis's arms.

Zach's eyelids pulled down, snapped open, then closed again.

Before the lights turned out for good, Zach muttered, "I'm...not into...kinky shtuff..."

"'...kinky stuff.' Then...I must've passed out."

"That's all you remember, Zach? Nothing else? Did you get a last name from this 'Cat'?"

"No. I don't think so."

"And can I say...ew. Just... *ew*."

"What? Hey, it's how I roll."

"Yeah…keep on rolling."

"I killed the song, though, didn't I?"

"You butchered it."

Zach smiled, proud of his sister's rare compliment.

"Another dead end street, Zach."

"But…we got a name for the chauffeur. Dennis." Zach smiled, still amused by the freaky chauffer's name.

"Sure, that's great. We'll just go look up every Dennis in Kansas City."

"I'm just sayin, that's all."

"Fine. I'll figure something out. But I've gotta get the kids to Mom and Dad's first."

"Oh, yeah…dropping the kids off." Like he needed *that* reminder.

"We're going to Grandma and Grandpa's! We're going to Grandma and—"

"Justin, if you don't stop shouting, you won't be going. Capiche?"

"Ka peace."

"Mom, why don't we see Grandma and Grandpa more often?" asked Nikki.

Frankly, Zach was fine with seeing them about three times a year: Christmas, Thanksgiving and an annual funeral of some distant relative he'd never heard of before.

"That's kinda hard to answer, honey," said Zora. "Sometimes adults have their differences."

"Huh."

"Zora, I know we need to get the kids to safety and everything, but—"

"What do we need to be safe from, Mom? From the guy who chased us?"

"—tell me again, why we have to go see Mom and Dad."

Zora sighed, long and weighty. "We can't take them with us, Zach! Your play-pals are chasing us!"

"Well, yeah, duh. But, like, why not just get a babysitter or something?"

"Oh, really? *Really?* So, tell me parent-of-the-year, how'm I supposed to get a babysitter at the last moment? For three kids?" With her hands on the wheel, she glared at Zach. A little too long for his comfort. Especially after the whirlwind ride they'd just survived.

"Um...eyes on the road, sis."

"Don't tell me how to drive! My kids have already scared off most of the local babysitters." She whipped her head around, gave her kids a bitter smile. A scary smile Zach had been on the receiving end of many times. "Precious little monsters. Anyway, as it is, if Phillip wants to go out on the town, we have to set up something months in advance. Our parents are a last resort."

"Maybe they're not home." *Wishful thinking*.

"Zach, when have you ever known them *not* to be home? Dad's few clients come out to their...'farm,' while Mom...does whatever it is she does. Putters around in their fields, living off the land. Hippy crap."

"Growing their weed," Zach added quietly. Just not quietly enough.

"*What?* Grandma and Grandpa do *drugs*?" hollered Nikki.

"Way to go, Zach. No, honey...um, it's for medicinal purposes."

Zach snorted. "Yep, medicinal purposes, sure."

"Anyway...no, I don't agree with their lifestyles. That's why we don't visit often. But this is a special occasion, kids!" Zach admired his sister's effort at putting a positive spin on the situation. Too bad she couldn't manage some spin control for him. "You'll enjoy your visit."

"Just don't get in the hot tub with them."

"Zach!"

"Sorry, kids, crap, sorry."

Growing up, Zach dreaded the family "communal baths." Dad had read something about Japanese families taking baths together, so in his hippy way, he thought of it as getting back to nature. Naked, of course. Usually, Zach liked to reserve his nudity for the dance stage. Normal stuff. But definitely not cool for family time.

Zach turned around, put a hand beside his mouth, and stage-whispered, "Really, though, guys...don't get in the hot tub."

He couldn't believe his sister chuckled. But he always could make her laugh. It sounded good, the first moment of relief they'd had all day.

"Got it, no hot tubs," said Nikki.

"No hot tubs," sang Justin.

"Good Gawd," said Zora.

"Hey, um, sis?"

"What?"

"You mind if I stay in the car? When you take the kids inside?"

For a second, Zora's foot hit the brake, jerking them forward. "Oh no. Ohhh no! You've got to be kidding me! It's because of your big, stupid, sloppy mess—"

"I'm not sloppy."

"...that we're going out there in the first place! I'm not about to take this on by myself!

Besides...you're the golden boy. Can't do any wrong in Mom and Dad's eyes. While they thought I was a 'sell-out to the Man' when I landed my security gig. Whereas you...you...gah!"

"Just a thought."

"A first."

"But, you know, really...Mom and Dad, um, think I work with the Kansas City Ballet. It's hard enough coming up with excuses all the time why they can't come see me perform."

"Yeah...wouldn't that be an eye-opener?"

"Oh, whatever. Maybe I should just tell them the truth. They've always prided themselves on being cool leftwing hippies. They'd probably understand. Maybe even appreciate my artistry."

Zora guffawed, droplets of spit smacking the windshield. "Yeah, sure, why not? Your 'artistry.' Maybe you can give Mom a lap-dance."

"Gross, sis."

"Mommy, what's a lap dance?"

"Something that's demeaning and gross and should be illegal, sweetheart."

"What's dem-een—"

"Never mind. The grown-ups are talking. Yeah, Zach, our parents always claim they're liberals. But the only thing 'left' about them is their limbs. And their penchant for communal baths and weed. At heart, they're as conservative as they come."

"Whatever…" Zach screeched a finger down the passenger window. Not to be left out of the fun, Justin conducted finger music on his window.

"Stop it, Justin."

Screeee-tump…

"I just sometimes think my life would be easier if I could level with them, sis. You know, lay it out there, as Dad used to say."

"Okay…first of all, if your life's so hard, it's because you make it that way. With your choices."

"What's wrong with my choices?"

"Well, I dunno, let's see…hmm, have you forgotten the mess you're in?"

"Not my fault."

"Oh, for… If you weren't a…" She put up annoying finger quotes and lowered her voice.

"…'male dancing entertainer,' none of this crap would've ever happened."

"You just don't understand."

"That's right. I just don't understand. You know what I do understand?"

"What?"

"Shut up, that's what."

On the outskirts of town, Zora whipped the van into a desolate convenience store parking lot. Apparently a last minute decision. Maybe she'd been doing a few too many last minute decisions behind the wheel recently.

"What're we doing here?"

"I'm gonna get the kids something to eat. Before we drop them off. You remember what Mom's food's like."

How could he forget? "Ugh. Yeah." Raised on a diet of trendy, home-grown, barely edible food, Zach vowed once he left home he'd only eat healthy. As long as it tasted good. Couldn't ever figure out how Spam fit into his parents' health-minded crusade, though. The thought of that phony canned meat made him want to hurl. Again.

"Mommy, can I get candy?"

"No. Zach…I'm leaving Samantha with you. Think you can handle it?"

He laughed. "Yeah, I'm great with babies. Besides…she's still asleep, right? Right?" He turned around, checking on her. Yep, still asleep. *Whew.*

"Sure, great with babies. Uh-huh. You ever even held one?"

"What? Of course." *Nope. Never.* "Lots of 'em. Lots and lots and lots."

"Okay, fine, baby whisperer." After Zora let out Nikki and Justin, she opened Zach's door. Clumped the diaper bag into his lap. "She's due for a diaper change."

"Wait…what?"

Zora and the kids had already skated halfway to the store. Walking backward, Zora smiled. *Smiled.* Her inner sadist showing. But maybe he deserved the treatment. For dragging her and the kids into it. Just a little.

Before Zora entered the store, she called back, "Don't screw it up!"

Pfft. Right. Like I could screw up changing a diaper. No way am I gonna screw this up. No way!

"Alright, Samantha, let's do this."

Zach whipped up her seat, carried her to the back of the minivan. He needed the elbow room to work, man on a mission. With the carrier down, he lifted Samantha out. Holding her aloft, he sniffed at her diaper, grimaced. Samantha squirmed, wriggling in his hands. Smiling like her mother, the entire family out to make his life a living hell. But still freakishly quiet. Before he dropped her, which wouldn't go over well at all with her mother, he laid her down.

Procrastinating.

"Okay, Sam…diapers, diapers…" He rummaged through the bag, snagged a diaper.

"You're packing a full load, girl." He peeled off the tape at one side of the diaper, folded it back. The smell alone could've stopped an elephant dead in its tracks. Fighting his gag reflex, he removed the diaper.

"Man, Sam, what've you been eating?" Things shouldn't look that green. And should there be so much? Hard to think it came out of her, practically half of her body weight.

Sam waggled her feet as he set the used diaper beside her. But the job seemed incomplete.

He rifled through the diaper bag, grabbed a plastic container.

Wet wipes! Always wondered what they were for.

Zach pulled out a thick handful of the wipes, a decent-sized barrier between his hand and the unspeakable.

"Just hang in there, Sam. This is gonna hurt me a lot more than you." He darted in, dabbed, pulled away fast. Even though she was still dirty, Sam smiled at him.

This is a lot more work than I thought.

"Okay, Sammy, let's stop messing around." Gently, he lassoed one of Sam's wiggling legs, held his breath, shut his eyes and patted down the baby's bottom.

Zach exhaled, examined his work, smiled.

Yep, good as new.

The new diaper's tape caught on his finger, then latched onto another part of the material. The diaper bag's promise of "EZ use" was a downright lie. Have to be a brain surgeon to figure it out.

Behind him, headlights flashed, rose up into the trees. Tires crunched over gravel. The car stopped, its motor still ticking.

Zach turned.

Crap.

Black caddy. New dent in the back. And tall, dark and gruesome stepped out of the car: Dennis, Cat's menace.

Crap. Crap. Crap.

Silently, the chauffer glided toward Zach. Grinning, displaying a shark's worth of white teeth.

EZ Brite goes on quick, tastes so good, just give it a lick...

No! Focus!

Zach swept up Samantha in one arm, wielding the filled diaper in the other hand. "Get back! I've got a diaper! And I'm not afraid to use it."

The chauffer stopped. Zach met his pale blue gaze, standing his ground. Then the tall man grabbed Zach's arm and squeezed, a show of strength. "You're coming with me."

"Dude, get off me!" Zach shrugged him loose, whirled. Brought up the diaper.

Splat. A perfect landing.

Stunned, Dennis staggered back, his hands clawing at his face. Screaming as if he'd been burned. Only far worse.

The chauffer rebounded, reeled back, swung. Zach ducked, Samantha tucked against his belly. A double punch whooshed over Zach's head.

Zach danced back, a boxer's taunt. He planted the ball of his foot, pivoted, kicked the other leg up. Rolling it out kick boxer style. Part of his rigid dancing training.

His foot caught the much larger man in the chest. Dennis stumbled backward, arms flailing for balance. Gravity won the day, dropping him to the cement. Zach seized the moment, ran at him with Samantha cradled in his arms like a football. He leaped. Another kick to the chauffer's face, one for the road. He went flat on his back, out.

"Zach!" Zora barreled out of the store, her purse slung over her shoulder, gun pointed up. Nikki and Justin scrambled behind her, trying to keep up. Freaking out over their pistol-packing mama.

"Mommy's got a gun!"

"What the hell, Zach?"

"Mommy cussed!"

"This is the guy, Zora! Cat's driver. The guy who's been following us!"

"Great. Did you have to kill him? With a diaper?"

"Dead guys don't snore like that. Pretty cool, right?"

Zora looked over her shoulder into the store window. The clerk was on the phone, his hands waving flags of panic. Big day at Convenience Quick.

"No, there's nothing cool about any of this!" Zora grabbed Samantha, gave her a quick check-out. "Come on…we've got to get outta here before the cops come." She glanced at the Caddy, frowned. Handed Samantha back to her brother. "Get the kids in the car. Fast. I gotta do something. And put her diaper on, for God's sake. Can't trust you to do anything."

"I was kinda busy, you know, trying not to get killed and everything."

"Whatever. Move!" Zora hustled away, as fast as an eight month pregnant woman could.

Squatting next to the Caddy, she pointed the gun at the tire.

Bang! Tsssss...

"Whoa!" she said. "Now *that's* cool."

———————

"Sis, how come this guy keeps finding us?" asked Zach.

Something bugged Zora, fingernails scratching down the board of her brain.

Crap. Stupid.

"Give me your phone."

"Why? You already said there's nothing—"

"Just give it to me!"

Reluctantly, he handed it over. Acting like it was his prized possession. Probably was, too, other than his banana speedo.

She heaved the phone out the window.

"Mom, you littered!"

"Hey! Dang it, that's my phone!"

"Get another. Think about it for a minute, Stephen Hawking. You—"

"Who's Stephen Hawking? Some famous male dancer or—"

"Not important! You asked how the big chauffer found us. We tracked down your phone, right?"

He nodded. His dim bulb sparked to life. "Oh. You think that he did the same—"

"I know he did. Only thing that makes sense."

"Well, crap...all my numbers were in there."

"It's not like you're hard to find, Zach. Anyone who wants your phone number can find you at your gross club."

"I guess...but it took me a long time to get all those—"

"Oh, whatever, like you're gonna go on a date tonight."

He shrugged. Gave her a forlorn look. Mumbled, "First my pants, then my phone…" Bad day for her brother. Worse for Zora.

"You know, if you didn't knock out the driver, we might've learned something."

He flexed a muscle. Kissed it. "What can I say? I'm a force of nature."

"Force of something, maybe."

"Don't I know it."

Clueless. Absolutely clueless. Zora wondered how her brother'd gotten along all of his so-called adult life without her. Not very well, judging from today's events.

Justin let out a screech of excitement when they pulled onto her parents' gravel driveway. Not much had changed since her last visit. Fields of corn and other produce, including, presumably, a hidden marijuana patch, surrounded the ramshackle country house. Their ludicrous van—still running after all these years—sat next to the outdoor cellar, a hideous lava-lamp of swirling neons and a new lovely shade of rust.

Welcome to the funny farm.

Zach looked like he might shriek, too, just not of the excitement-filled variety. The only one who dreaded these visits more than Zora. But her children's safety came first.

"Come on, brother, chin up. You've faced a dead senator, a plastic sex kitten and a giant killing machine. Can't be all that bad."

"Whatever."

Justin and Nikki had already exited the minivan, soaring toward the front door. Zora and Zach trudged along behind them.

"Let's just get this over with, Zach."

Zora's mother opened the door and threw her arms wide. The children clung to her, tugging at her apron.

"Hi Grandma!"

"What a lovely surprise! How're my little angels?"

Yeah, right. Just wait 'til you watch 'em for a while, Mom.

"You should've called first," said Sunshine, looking over her grandchildren's heads.

"Hey, Mom. It's not like you ever answer your land-line. And you don't have a cell phone."

"Now, Zora, you know how they cause brain cancer. Zach! You're looking well!"

"Hi, Mom." Zach leaned in, pecked her cheek and got out fast.

"And all dressed up in a suit…big interview? Or a hot date?" She nudged her son with an elbow, added a wink.

"You know me, Mom, dressing for success." Zora rolled her eyes. Not that either her mother or brother noticed. Too wrapped up in each other, the way family visits always go.

"Mom, I know it's short notice…but could you watch the kids for a while? Maybe the night?"

Sunshine's brow wrinkled, her usual look. Too many years spent distrusting "The Man."

"Sure…I guess. Kinda unusual, though…given we haven't babysat in a long time."

"It's important, Mom."

"Where are my manners, come in, come in." She waved them in.

"Thought I heard voices!"

Not the first time Dad's heard voices either.

Zora's father came strutting in, his bow-legged prowl more noticeable than last year. His wardrobe hadn't been updated, though. Overalls over a tie-dyed t-shirt, a matching accessory to their van, pure hippy chic. And his hair, that damn hair. A long gray ponytail hanging from his bald pate. Bald men shouldn't wear ponytails, just common sense. It constantly surprised Zora her father had a successful psychiatric practice.

"Hey there, kids!" Kelp—he'd legally changed his name in the Seventies from Robert—bent over, hands on knees. "How's Nikki? Pretty as a picture, I see. And Justin…Justin, hey kiddo, pull my finger!" He prodded his index finger toward Justin, poking him in the chest. "Go on, pull it. Come on, kiddo, pull my finger." Ever since he went Vegan back in the Eighties, Zora's dad had turned into a bag of foul-smelling odors, able to dredge them up on command. She flashed back on her first day away at college, where she gorged herself on all matters of meat at an all-you-can-eat buffet. The indigestion had been well worth it. The taste of freedom.

"Go on, I won't bite. Pull my finger, Justin!"

Zach gave his nephew a covert look, shook his head, mouthed, *no*.

Obviously disappointed, Kelp straightened. "Right on, right on. Zach, son, how're you?" He leaned in for a hug.

Uncomfortable in his ill-fitting suit and skin, Zach obliged, putting a soul hand shake between their chests. Afraid to have their father's hippy ways rub off on him.

"Doing great, Dad."

"Grandpa," shouted Justin. "Mommy shot out a tire and we ran a stoplight and Beary Brian's chasing us and Uncle Zach beat up a guy with a diaper and—"

"That's enough, Justin." Zora moved in, her hands on Justin's shoulders. Ready to strangle if necessary. "You know how he is, Dad. With his wild imagination."

"Heh. Sure do. Always got your head in the clouds, don't ya, Justin?"

"But it really happened, Grandpa! It really—"

"This isn't the time, Justin." Zora's hand went over her son's mouth. Bored already, presumably with the unfathomable world of adults, Justin shrugged, dropped it. "Grown-ups are talking."

On tiptoes, Kelp looked out through the door. "Where's little Sammy? Where's the girl?"

"Ah! She's still in the van," said Zora. "Forgot all about her."

"Here, let Grandpa get her." Still spry for his years, Kelp raced out the door at a sprinter's pace. He came back in swinging the car seat dangerously high. Of course Samantha slept through it all.

"Dad! Here…give her to me before you send her flying. She's sleeping!"

"Hm? Oh, sure, little gal could sleep in the eye of a tornado." Kelp set the seat on the floor. "Come on in…pop a squat."

Zora sighed, shook her head. Her father's fondness for keeping up on modern slang annoyed the living hell out of her.

"Dad, we can't stay long. We've got something we—"

"Oh, horse pucky! Hardly see you kids at all. Surely you got a little bit of time for your ol' folks."

Zora checked her watch, made it obvious. Best way to counter her dad's guilt game. "We really need to—"

"Come on in, come on in!"

Zach shrugged, followed their mother. Resigned, Zora joined them. Arguing with her parents was an exercise in futility, stretching out the smallest of decisions into long-ranging wars. She'd spare them five minutes and they were gone.

In the living room, Sunshine had already settled into her beanbag. Most parents have "ma and pa recliners." Not the Caulfields. Relics of an ancient generation, they proudly held onto their matching beanbags, patches and all.

The air whiffed out of Kelp's beanbag as he plunged into it. "Now...what's the purpose of your visit?" No longer the host with the amiable most, Kelp settled into his serious shrink-face, all concerned wrinkles and authoritative extended lower lip. "Must be something serious."

Nikki was growing antsy, walking around in a circle. Justin stood beside her, bouncing on his sneakers, doing a bathroom dance. Time to release the beasts.

"Kids, why don't you go outside and play?"

They ran to their grandfather, hopping up and down. "Can we go play in the fields, Grandpa? Can we?"

"Sure, kids, why not?" He unleashed them with a wave, allowing them free rein through his fields of weed.

"Uh...don't touch anything kids," shouted Zora. "Okay, Mom...Dad..." Zora tried on a serious face, too. It didn't hold. Even though she'd faced down thugs and gun-toting criminals in the past, her parents always had the ability to reduce her to a little girl, shy and withdrawn. She sat on the sofa next to her brother, gathering her thoughts. Leaned back to relieve her aching back, stuck her legs out. Studied them. Seriously buying time. "I know I don't ask you to babysit much—"

"Ever," interjected Sunshine with an imperious finger.

"Not true. But I'm in a bit of a jam here and I hate calling on you last second, but I really—"

"Are you in some kind of trouble?" Kelp leaned forward, digging for his wallet. He always offered money first even though he preached that hugs solve everything. Zora wished a hug could solve their current predicament.

Zach sat up, excited, practically licking his lips. Zora jabbed him with an elbow.

"Dad! Put your money away! You know Phillip and I are doing fine. We—"

"Oh, yes. *Phillip.*" Ice dripped from Kelp's lips as he slowly enunciated Zora's husband's name. Worst thing in the world to an aging hippy? Accountants. "Well…fine. What about you, Zach, the Kansas City Ballet paying you what you're worth?" The beanbag scrunched as Kelp shifted again, second excavation attempt at his always full wallet. Because banks were strictly forbidden in the Caulfield household. The evils of corporate America and all.

"Well, come to think of it, Dad, I could use—"

"Say no more, say no more." He pinched out two twenties, raised his eyebrows. A trap.

Another nudge to her brother set him back into the sofa.

"It's not about money. I just need you to babysit the kids, for God's sake. Please."

With great drama, Kelp whipped his wire-rimmed glasses off, set them on his knee. Put a finger over his lip and tapped it. The doctor was in! "I…see. Now, let's lay it all on the table, shall we? What I'm seeing here bothers me. We don't see you two in months, you drop in unexpectedly with the kids. Together. Odd. Let's rap, kids, adult to adult. How 'bout you level with the old man, rap with him and…"

Oh, for God's sake. We're never getting outta here!

Kelp rambled on, Zora's mind drifting to more urgent concerns. When her Dad was on the shrink seat, he loved to hear himself talk, the only one in the room. She lifted her wrist, made a grand performance out of checking the time. Maybe this had been a huge mistake. But, really, what other choice did she have?

"Zach!" Abruptly, Sunshine clapped her hands, bringing Zora back to the room. "We've been dying to see you perform!" Sometimes, Zora thought her mom interrupted her father intentionally to shut him up. Very subtly, very smoothly.

Way to go, Mom!

"Ah...you know...I'm sorry, but I've told you how I get...stage fright if someone I love is in the audience. I might mess up and not put on a good show." Zach offered outstretched goodwill hands and his charming smile. The parents weren't buying it. Even though they didn't have time for this, Zora's mouth curled up at the corner. Fighting a mad smirk. Her brother deserved to squirm a little bit.

"Oh, but that's silly, Zach," said Zora. "Since there's no one here except for Mom and Dad, why don't you give them a little preview of what you can do?"

He gave Zora a round-eyed look, leaning somewhere between shock and stark fear.

Dance, pretty boy, dance!

"I think that sounds like a rockin' good idea," yelled Kelp, thankfully abandoning his Dr. Caulfield guise. "Come on, son!"

"Yeah, come on, Zach!" Zora slapped her hands on his back, pushing him until he had no choice but to stand.

"Well...I...ah, usually need some...um, classical music to dance to." He ran a hand through his full head of hair, grinning, believing he'd dodged the bullet.

"Got your needs covered, Zach." Sunshine reached toward the small coffee table between her and Kelp, fiddled with something. Chords of Beethoven filled the room, blasting from a small, yellow iPod. Their first concession to modernization in years. One Zach clearly hadn't counted on.

This is gonna be good!

Guilt bit into Zora. Well, more like nibbled. Sadistic? Sure, of course. But funny? Absolutely!

With no way out, Zach thrust his arms in front of him, clenched his fists. Did minor knee-bends, shaking his hands, killing time. Searching for a beat. Classical music was poison to Zach, had been forever. He much preferred his steady diet of ghastly arena rock and metal. For minutes, he bounced on bent knees, his legs planted like an awkward kid at his first school dance.

Kelp slipped a questioning glance toward Sunshine, but she had her golden-boy blinders on, entranced by Zach's ludicrous routine. Zora put a hand over her mouth, hiding a grin. Didn't really matter. All eyes were on her brother's floundering about, hypnotically so.

"Um, son?" Kelp raised his voice to be heard over the music. "Is that…what they're teaching you at the KC Ballet?"

"Yeah, Dad!" Loosening up a bit (no doubt to the rock blaring in his head), Zach swayed back and forth, swinging his arms behind him, in front of him. Smacking his hands together.

"I'm just warming up!"

Uh-oh. Maybe another one in a long line of bad ideas I've had today.

Beaming like her name's sake, Sunshine's face crinkled up. Her hands clasped together as if in prayer. So proud of her son. Zora had a feeling that pride would soon be put to the test.

Her brother's body flowed into liquid, a rolling and undulating wave. His eyes closed, apparently sinking into his stripper zone. He raised a foot, twirled on his other. Smacked his rear, screeched, "Yeah! That's what I'm *talkin'* about!"

Kelp sat forward, mouth gaping open through his bush of a beard. The smile fell a little from Sunshine's face, not much. Still her golden boy.

Zach continued the torture, apparently oblivious now to his whereabouts. At least he kept his clothes on. Small favors. He twirled, kicked a leg up high. When he turned his back on them and bent at the waist, Zora really worried.

Don't go there, don't go there, don't go…

Not only did he go there, but he let his ass lead him. With hands on his knees, he shook his bottom, twerking as if his life depended on it. Zora covered her eyes. She preferred a dangerous car chase.

Oh my God, so stupid! Please make it stop!

God heard her prayers, granted her mercy. Zach straightened, twisted one last time. Raised a victory fist and shouted, "Yeah!"

Kelp reached over and thumbed off the iPod. Zach's panting, his chest heaving in and out, filled the room. Otherwise, radio silence.

Sunshine shifted, the beanbag crunching beneath her. She exchanged a look with her husband. Then Zora's mother clapped. A slow clap at first, straight out of an annoying sports movie. Then Kelp joined her.

You've got to be kidding me!

"Son...I've gotta say..." Kelp levered himself out of his beanbag and went toward Zach, arms out. "...wasn't what I was expecting at all. But it's mighty impressive, mighty impressive. You've got some mad skills, some mad moves!"

"Well, of course he does, Kelp!" Sunshine joined the group love moment. "Naturally, he's talented! He's a Caulfield, after all!"

While they hugged it out, Zora sat on the sofa. Stunned. And not a Caulfield. Now a married LeFevre.

She couldn't take it, not any longer. Crap to do, places to go, idiot stripper brothers to save. She rolled off the sofa to her knees then climbed to her feet.

"Well, Kumbaya and all that! Huzzah for Zach! Thanks for babysitting. We've got to go."

They didn't hear her. Not over Zach's ridiculous bragging and lying.

"At the KC Ballet, they make sure we know all kinds of...dance stuff."

"I thought I recognized you twerking. That was a twerk, right?"

"Oh, yeah, I know it all. You should see my other moves."

"Love too, anytime, son."

"How 'bout if I—"

A two fingers in the mouth whistle stopped the love fest. The next best thing to pulling the gun out and blasting holes in the ceiling. "Hey! Zach, we've got to go!"

"Oh, yeah, yeah...right, sis."

The loving hands of her parents dropped from their stripper son. But Dr. Caulfield, professionally serious shrink, was back on the job again. He transferred his hands to Zora's shoulders.

In a quiet voice, he said, "Zora. I feel you're in trouble. It doesn't make sense, your showing up here with your brother. Especially when he's dressed in a suit. One that obviously belongs to your husband."

She wanted to scream. Even in his fatherly moments with her, it was still all about Zach. "Phillip, Dad. My husband's name is Phillip."

"Of course it is, honey. But...can you tell me what kind of trouble you're in, Zora? Lay it on the line, get down and—"

"Dad...no. I don't have time now. Okay? Just...trust me. Please?"

He smiled, a sad, small smile. Then he nodded. "I do trust you, honey. And I love you." Dipping in, he brushed her cheek with a kiss.

"Love you too, Dad."

Not done yet—he was never done when it came to touchy-feely moments—Kelp whispered into Zora's ear, "Take care of your brother, alright? You've always been the sensible one. Cool?"

It floored Zora. He'd never told her that before. And maybe he'd been paying more attention to her than he'd let on before. No matter, no time for maudlin moments. She returned his kiss, said, "Cool, Dad."

Chapter Six

Yeah, thanks, sis." Zach couldn't believe Zora did it. Maybe he could. But he didn't like it. "Thanks a helluva lot."

"What're you talking about?" Innocent words, sure, but Zach judged her guilty, guilty, *guilty* based on her sly smile .

"You set me up. Made me dance for Mom and Dad."

"Me? Mom's the one who asked you to do it."

"Yeah, but you egged her on."

"Like you ended up with egg on your face. You still came out smelling like a friggin' rose."

He flashed his teeth, gave his dimples a workout. "I killed it, didn't I? Like I always do."

"You know, today you gotta quit saying you 'killed' things."

"Oh, yeah, right."

She shook her head, mumbled, "Can't believe you twerked in front of Mom."

"Alright, I think we need to drop it now." In retrospect, it did seem kinda hard to believe. But he'd been in the moment, feeling the rush of dancing. When things like that grab you, you gotta grab back. He wondered if he should put his epiphany on a bumper-sticker. Maybe write a self-help book.

"Drop it like it's hot, you mean?"

"Okay, okay... You know, I almost told them I'm a male entertainment dancer and—"

"A stripper."

"Male entertainment dancer. I mean, it would've been the perfect time to tell them. Finally get it off my chest."

"Like your tear-away shirt?"

"I'm not gonna get anywhere with you, today, am I?"

"Probably not."

Still sitting in their parents' driveway, Zora finagled her seat belt around her eight month package. Took her forever.

"Now be quiet while I call Phillip."

Phillip. Kinda an okay guy, Zach supposed. A little pudgy, though, and as uptight as a popsicle on a stick. It didn't help that Phillip made it known he didn't care for Zach. Couldn't really figure out why, either. Sure, there was the mishap with his car that one time. Water under the bridge. Guy could hold a grudge. Honestly, Zach sometimes wondered what his sister saw in him.

"Hi honey, it's me."

Squawking came out the other end, sounding like Charlie Brown's teacher. Just higher-pitched, whiny in that grating Phillip fashion.

"I know you're busy… Hey, watching your kids isn't a cakewalk… I know, I know…"

She used her pacifying tone, one she didn't even use on her kids.

"The reason I'm calling… No, I know I don't need to have a reason to call… Love you, too…"

When Zach fluttered his eyes, Zora punched him.

"Ow!"

"Huh?… Oh, nobody, just my brother…Yes, Phillip, I know, I know… He says he'll pay to get the car fixed…"

Zach smiled, feigned playing a violin.

"Anyway…I just dropped the kids off at my parents…"

Phillip's squawk grew into a rooster's crow.

"Phillip LeFevre!"

Uh-oh. Her mad mom voice.

"How 'bout you come home and watch them for a change?… I know you're working! And speaking of work, we're gonna have a long talk about that when I get home!… No, I'm not going to talk about it now! I've got something important I have to take care of… Yes, with

71

Zach and my parents were the only ones I could get on short notice! I told them no drugs, no hot tubs—"

"No pulling the finger jokes," added Zach.

"Yes, they understand!" Zora held the phone up to God. Drummed her fingers over the steering wheel. Took a few deep breaths, probably something she learned in Lamaze class. Returned with her indoor voice. "It's just something important I have to do… No, he hasn't gotten me into trouble…" Although the look she gave Zach told a different story.

"Let me talk to him, sis. I'll clear things up." Zach nodded, a firm believer in his own dignitary abilities. Zora gave him an eye-roll, her eye muscles really getting a workout today.

"I can't get into that now. I'll explain everything when I see you…When?… I have no idea. But you're probably gonna be on your own for dinner… You've got to be kidding me! There're plenty of leftovers in the frig. Figure it out! You're not a helpless little baby bird!… Meatloaf, there's meatloaf! You know how to work the microwave, never stopped you from making your God-awful nachos on Sundays!.. Tough it out!… Look, I gotta go. Love you, too, dammit!"

Zora slapped the phone off, a stand-in for Phillip, and tossed it to Zach. She strangled the air with trembling hands. Best to let her ride her mood out and stay quiet. Either that or have those strangling hands wrapped around his neck.

"What is it with you men? Can't do a damn thing on your own!" Zach figured she really didn't want an answer. "And now that my kids are gone, I'm gonna cuss! *Goddam, son* of a…"

It went on for a while. Zach tried to put on an understanding face, one he'd learned from Dad. When the smoke finally cleared, Zora fired up the minivan.

"Alright…look up Senator Hal Turlington on my phone."

Zach's finger flew over the keyboard. Lots of hits. "What're we looking for?"

"Does it say if he was married?"

"No… Wait, here's a story…he and his wife, Ingrid, went to some fundraising deal. Something about schools or something…"

"Is there a picture of her?"

"No. Why?"

"Hasn't it crossed your mind she might be 'Cat'?"

"Oh, right! The wife always does it."

"That your expert opinion, Zach?"

"Well, yeah, I've read a lotta books and—"

"Ahem!"

"Fine. I've watched a lotta TV."

"Any photos, Sherlock?"

"No…nope…nothing. Just pictures of Turlington. He looks a lot different when he's alive."

"Very astute observation."

"Now what?"

"Find an address for the late senator."

"Got it! They live in Mission Hills."

"Figures. Where all the rich live in Kansas City."

"So…what're we gonna do?"

"We're going to pay Mrs. Turlington a visit."

Usually, Zora had great ideas. The reason Zach turned to her. But this one sounded…not so great. "Um…she's gonna be, like, grieving and everything. Do we really have to—"

"You wanna clear your name? Get you back in your golden sack?"

"Well, yeah, but—"

"Then that's where we're going."

"Why don't we just go to the hotel and ask the clerk if—"

"If he recognizes you? And calls the cops! Think, Zach! The cops are probably still crawling all over that place!"

"Gotcha."

"We'll be lucky enough if the cops aren't still visiting the widow Turlington."

Zach sank into his seat. Swallowed a dry lump, thinking about bumping into the cops. Again, not one of his sister's best ideas.

EZ Brite, people will notice, EZ Brite puts you in focus…

———————

"Okay, again, the only reason you're going with me is because detectives always travel in pairs. Keep your mouth shut, let me do the talking."

Zach locked his lips, pitched the imaginary key. Zora gave him a long, hard stare-down.

"Sis, I'm not a kid. You don't have to keep telling me things over and over and—"

"Yeah, not sure about that. Look, Zach, at the Hot Beef Injection Club, you're—"

"Bone-in Beef Club."

"Like it matters! At your sleazy joint—"

"Not sleazy."

"...you might be king, but we're playing on my turf now. Just follow my lead." And, again, it felt good to be king again. If the stakes weren't so high, Zora would be enjoying herself. Immensely.

Flipping through her cards in the wallet, she found what she needed. A phony detective ID along with a toy badge. If you studied it, it looked clearly fake. But it'd been her experience that people rarely gave police identification more than a cursory glance, particularly when flashed for a second. Generally, people are so freaked out by cops visiting, they take police identification for granted. The badge had come in handy during her days in the field which seemed like a lifetime ago. She didn't know why she'd kept it but was glad she did. For easy access, she tucked it into her jacket pocket.

"Do I get a badge?"

"No. Shut up."

Foreign sports cars filled the driveways of the Mission Hills mansions, candy of the rich. The Turlington mansion was no exception, a Ferrari, newly waxed and washed, parked at the top of the hill. Three other cars were lined up behind it on the street-worthy length of a driveway. As they walked by the cars, Zora peeked through the windows. None of them appeared to be police cars. No police radios, caged backseats, other dead giveaways. Dodged that bullet and Zora was more than happy to keep dodging them.

For once, Zach had been right about one thing, though. It bothered her to call on a grieving widow under false pretenses. As pissed as she got at Phillip at times, it'd piss her off even more if someone pulled a stunt like that on her. Then again, she meant to bring the senator's killer to justice. A worthy con.

The English Tudor home seemed out of place, stuck in Kansas. But when compared to the neighboring homes, it fit in nicely enough, nestled between houses of different styles and European touches. A residential Epcot Center.

Zora rang the doorbell set next to the lavish French doors.

The door opened. A man dressed in a gray three-piece suit, not typical servant wear, looked at them with passive eyes behind trendy square-rimmed glasses. "May I help you?"

"Hope so. I'm Detective Laura Jones with the KCMO police..." Quick flash and back to her pocket. "This is my partner—"

"Detective David Hassle...berg."

Dammit. Can't take him anywhere.

She would've jabbed Zach, but the man watched them with the fervor of a scientist. Unblinking eyes. Stolid face. A wax dummy.

Zora reclaimed the train of her investigation before it derailed. "I know it's a bad time for Mrs. Turlington, but we'd like to ask her a few questions."

"The police have already been here. Mrs. Turlington is resting. Heavily medicated, as you may imagine."

"I'm sure, Mr...." Zora waited. The man was slow in complying.

"I'm Senator Turlington's political advisor, Samuel Tufts."

He stared at her extended hand, then went back to checking out their admittedly odd detective's wardrobe. For a political advisor, Zora thought, he totally lacked in people skills.

"Mr. Tufts, I know it's an imposition, but we really need to speak to Mrs. Turlington."

Finally, a blink! Slow to raise his eyelids, he looked first at Zora, then at Zach. Nothing, expression of the dead.

"Please wait here while I look in on Mrs. Turlington to see if she's in any condition to receive callers."

The door closed. Zora heard him latch the lock. Not a very trusting man. Then again his boss was just murdered. Probably not too happy to be out of a job.

"What did I tell you about keeping your mouth shut, Zach?" Zora whispered.

"Hey, sorry, just seemed right to introduce myself."

"Yeah, idiot, this isn't the time to play out your Baywatch fantasies!" For a moment, his gaze wandered, a melancholy smile spreading across his lips. Literally fantasizing now, judging by the goofy look on his face. "For the final time, I'll do the talking. Just…nod on occasion or something. Think you can do that?"

He nodded. Fast learner.

Clack-rrrrch. The door pulled back. Mr. Personality stepped aside. Silently, he waved them in. Gave a small bow, all of his expression in his body, not his face.

"Follow me if you will, detectives."

Up they went around a winding staircase. Mouth-breathing in awe, Zach marveled at the sumptuous decorations, the impeccable craftsmanship of the architecture. Zora didn't blame him. The beautiful moldings and hardwood and tile floors were something she'd dreamed of. Someday, maybe.

On the second floor, Tufts tapped politely on double-doors. The sounds of an excited television news reporter drifted out. Tufts knocked louder.

"Mrs. Turlington, I have the detectives here," he called out, more animated than Zora'd seen him before.

"Come in." A strong voice, metal in her chords. Seemed to Zora like they breed politician's wives that way.

Like a butler, Tufts grabbed both door knobs, swung the doors inside. "These are detectives Jones and Hassleberg."

Zora expected a bed-ridden, doped out of her mind, winsome widow of a woman. Sometimes expectations should be kept in check. Standing in front of open balcony windows, Mrs. Turlington whirled, a movie star's entrance. The color of her silver hair, perfectly coiffed, usually denoted age. But on her, it fortified her with strength, a sturdy dignity. Handsome and becoming. Suddenly self-conscious, Zora patted down her hair, thinking she needed a do-over.

"Come in, detectives."

"Would you like me to stay, Mrs. Turlington?" asked Tufts.

She dismissed him with a cavalier toss of an elegant hand. "That's not necessary, Tufty."

If she'd been medicated, she hid it well. Except, of course, for the wine glass in her hand. Self-medicating. *Celebrating?* She crossed the room, snatched up a remote and muted the wall-covering television. Reporting the latest on her husband's murder. Always a politician's wife, thought Zora, keeping up on her media coverage.

"I thought I'd answered all of your questions earlier, detectives." Just like her husband's advisor, she thoroughly checked them out, eyes blatantly dropping and lowering over their clothes. Zora suddenly felt naked, ill-prepared. It'd been too long since she'd been in the field. "Why are you back to bother me in my moment of grief?"

Weird-ass way to show grief.

Zora looked for the tell-tale signs of grief: the puffy eyes, redness surrounding them. A hiccup in her voice. Weakness. Instead, Mrs. Turlington may as well've just left a day spa.

"I'm sorry to impose on you again, Mrs. Turlington. Especially at a time like this. But we have some follow-up questions."

Although there were plentiful loveseats and French chairs throughout the vast bedroom, she didn't offer them a seat. She didn't sit either, restlessly prowling in front of the balcony doors. "Follow up then." A regal hand went up. She whipped aside one half of her nearly floor length sweater and cocked a hip. "Detective Jones, is it?"

"Yes."

"Shouldn't you be on maternity leave?"

Zora smiled. She had a distinct feeling it was more of a smirk, though. Even women were sexist these days. "It's not my first rodeo, Mrs. Turlington. I plan on working 'til the little one drops."

"Admirable." *Slurrp.* A long drink of red wine. "And, you...the other one." She pointed a finger at Zach. Zach snapped to attention, shoulders back, chest out. Apparently he had no age limit when trying to impress women.

"Ma'am?"

"They're not paying you enough."

"Uh...I don't know what—"

"Your suit. Pocket's torn. And it doesn't fit you at all."

"Oh...ah...I've been on a diet."

Before Mrs. Turlington's interrogation continued, Zora charged in. "Mrs. Turlington...where were you last night between the hours of...eleven and two in the morning?"

She whipped out a notebook, one she'd confiscated earlier from her glove box. Beneath her grocery and "to do" list, she scribbled notes.

Get diapers, Nikki's play-date, murdered senator, callous widow...

"How is this a follow-up question, Detective?" For the first time, ire rose in her tone. At least Zora knew she was human. Better than apathy. Maybe she was medicated after all, perhaps used to living with it. Another perk of being a politician's wife. "I answered that earlier, more times than I cared to."

"Just one more time, Mrs. Turlington. Please."

She sighed. "Fine. I was home, of course. Sleeping. Where I'm supposed to be. Not like...not like..." Tears welled up. Her voice faltered. The iron woman rusted a bit. She flagged her hand at the on-going news report, let that finish her thought.

"Hey, now, ma'am." Zach started to go to her. Zora gripped his arm, held him back. Not the time for knight in shining armor crap.

The senator's widow recovered quickly and nicely. And very, very elegantly, damn her! A dainty fingertip to both eyes, a graceful quick swipe of her nose. She straightened again, composed, everything about her a glowing Grace Kelley moment. Zora looked down at her feet. Couldn't see them because of kid number four. She sighed.

"Again, I apologize for our intrusion, Mrs. Turlington. We're trying to find the person who did this to your husband. I know it's painful, but—"

"How many children do you have, Detective Jones?"

The question caught Zora off-guard. She lied, not sure why. "Two."

"We...I...have two, as well. One off to college, thank God. The other..." Another sniff, but she plugged it up. "...the other...still a child. In grade school. How do you think he'll react when I tell him...about his father?"

"Ah...I imagine it'll be very hard, Mrs. Turlington."

"Yes...yes, it will. And now...now, I'm left to raise him by myself."

Zora's thoughts scattered, playing out scenarios where she'd die, leaving Phillip to raise her kids. But she wouldn't let it happen, not in a million years. Not if she had anything to say about it. Even though not Catholic, Zora nearly crossed herself right there.

But she had to reclaim the room.

"Speaking as a mother, Mrs. Turlington, I can't imagine how hard it would be. My condolences. But, back to my question…and again, I apologize…"

What is it about her that makes me want to apologize? Friggin' woman should've been the senator, not her husband.

"Can anyone corroborate your being home asleep last night?"

"Oh, for Heaven's…well…" She chortled, one note, dry as a martini. "My husband could've…if he hadn't been…out sticking it into some whore. Or some man!"

"Um…I don't think your husband was gay, ma'am—"

Zora didn't care if Mrs. Turlington saw it or not. She stabbed an elbow into Zach's side. "I know this is a sensitive subject, but do you have any idea…who your husband was seeing?"

Again, she laughed. "I had no idea he was even having an affair! Not until today. With the reporters saying he was murdered in his love nest!"

"I don't think it was really a love nest—"

"Had you been getting along with your husband lately?"

"Define 'getting along.' We've been married for twenty-seven years! Twenty-seven years! All of the magic goes out of long-term marriages, a sad fact of life. But…I thought things were fine. Hal always…worked long hours. As a senator…it's expected. Foolish of me, really, not to have suspected anything, I suppose. For the last several years, we'd stopped sleeping together…"

Next to Zora, Zach shuffled. Drew a finger around his collar. Clearly uncomfortable discussing anyone else's sex life other than his own.

"I just thought it par for the course. I knew Hal's job could be…overwhelming at times. He took the burden of his constituents on as his own. Hal…oh, Hal…" She almost lost it again. But she rolled back her shoulders, took in a deep breath. Let it out. Grace under pressure. Or diverting Zora from her original question.

"Sorry to keep bothering you with this…but can anyone verify your being home last night? Staff, maybe?"

"Our staff is daytime only."

Must be nice.

"But, yes…as I told the other detectives…Mr. Tufts can verify I was here. Asleep."

Weird.

"Mr. Tufts, your husband's advisor?" Mrs. Turlington nodded. "Um…does he sleep here often?"

Mrs. Turlington dropped her shoulders, gave Zora an incredulous, less than graceful look: *Were you born stupid or did practice get you there?*

"Of course Tufty doesn't sleep here! Tufty couldn't find Hal. He had to talk to him about the upcoming primaries. Something that couldn't wait. So he waited downstairs for Hal while I went to bed."

"And how long was Mr. Tufts waiting last night?"

"I don't know…two, three in the morning before he gave up. I'm not sure. I was asleep. Ask him."

"We will. If you knew your husband was missing…weren't you worried? Did you try to call him?"

"Of course I did! Time and time again. So did Tufty. But Hal didn't answer…too busy…well…"

"I see. Sorry to bring it up again, Mrs. Turlington, but…and this is a prickly question, I know…but was the senator spending time with a woman friend? Maybe someone he worked with? Anyone you suspect?"

Zach swallowed, audible across the room. Mrs. Turlington raised an eyebrow, gave him a look before answering.

"I already told you, and the detectives before you, I didn't even have a clue he was having an affair."

"Maybe it wasn't an affair, ma'am, not really. Just a misunderstanding or something. I think—"

"Detective!" This time Zora didn't bother chastising her brother with physical violence. Her glare did the trick. "Sorry, Mrs. Turlington. We just have to be thorough, as I'm sure you understand."

"I suppose so."

"We're about wrapped up. One last question…do you have any idea who might've wanted to harm your husband? Did he have any enemies?"

This time her laughter sounded quite amused. Her tittering lasted longer than the moment merited. "Naturally Hal had enemies, as you so melodramatically put it. Or at least people he butted heads with. But, if you really want to find his killer, I'd start with whoever he was screwing last night."

"Believe me, ma'am, we're looking for her," said Zach.

One, two, three, four…

"You said Senator Turlington had political enemies. Who might they be?"

She crossed her arms, tapped a no-doubt-designer shoe. One that Zora imagined she could never afford. "You really haven't done your homework, have you, Detective Jones? As I said, the primaries are gearing up…" She pointed toward the muted TV. "There. Cleavon Smalls. Hal's biggest competition in the upcoming election."

On-screen, a rotund black man was shaking his head. Serious sad eyes. Spouting something in front of a microphone. The ticker at the bottom of the screen recapped clearly enough: *It's a shame a once beyond reproach man of high morals would use his power in office to procure…* A muck-raking opportunist. Welcome to the world of politics.

"Mr. Cleavon Smalls…" Zora wrote the name below "pick up Phillip's dry-cleaning. Got it. What can you tell me about Mr. Smalls?"

"Watch the news," she snapped. Then she held a hand over her eyes, shook her head. "I'm sorry, I must apologize for my outburst. It's been a trying time."

"Yes, I'm sure."

"But Hal and Smalls used to go head-to-head, using the media as their battle-ground. Things got nasty, accusations being flung left and right about teamsters, unions, crooked contracts…what have you. Politics."

"I see."

"If anyone had to gain anything from Hal's…murder, look no further than Smalls."

Zora glanced at Cleavon Smalls's image, raising a power fist and wearing a power tie, wondering if she was looking at a murderer.

"Thank you very much, Mrs. Turlington. I'm sorry to have imposed upon you in your time of grief. My deepest condolences for your loss."

Slucccck. She finished her glass of wine and headed for the bedside bar. With her back to them, pouring another glass, she said, "Please…just let me grieve."

"We'll see ourselves out, ma'am," said Zach, looking like he was ready to give her one of his brawny, feel-good hugs. Zora grabbed him, dragged him out of the room.

Suddenly appearing at the front door, Tufts gave Zora a start.

"Mr. Tufts!"

"Detective?" Eyes at half-mast, bored looking. Slip of a mouth, invisible lips.

"Mrs. Turlington says you were here most of the night."

"That's correct."

"What time did Mrs. Turlington go to bed?"

Without hesitation, "12:20."

"Uh-huh. And how long did you stay?"

"3:00 on the nose. Then I had to call it a night."

Which might explain his perpetually sleepy look. Or robotics could explain it.

"During that time, did Mrs. Turlington get up? Leave?"

"Absolutely not."

"Fine and dandy. We may have more questions for you later."

"I'll be here, tending to matters of business."

"I'm sure."

"Can I have one of your cards, Detective Jones?" A blip of a smile registered on his face. He held out an open palm, one that seemed void of lines. As smooth as his deadpan demeanor.

Crap. "Sorry, Mr. Tufts. Department cutbacks. We'll be in touch."

Zora turned, ready to hightail it to the van. She thought Zach was right behind her. Then she heard him talking to Tufts.

"…you really should smile more often, you know? Smiles are good, keeps wrinkles away. And you really oughta consider moisturizing. It's good—"

"Detective Hassleberg!"

As soon as they got in the van, Zora smacked her brother upside his head. Priorities.

"What the *hell*, sis? What was that for?"

"For being stupid, that's what! You almost said you were 'David Hasselhoff'! So dumb! Gah! Get over your stupid little juvenile infatuation, already!"

"The Hoff isn't stupid," he muttered. "Good actor. Hey, all those Germans can't be wrong."

"Oh, whatever." Zora stared down her brother until he looked away, shamed. Like a good dog. "So...I take it Mrs. Turlington wasn't your mystery woman."

"What? Hell no...I got better taste then that!"

"Yeah, right. I've seen some of your bimbos."

"They're not bimbos. Well...not all of them."

"Okay, so Mrs. Turlington and her man, Tufts, conveniently alibi one another."

"Well, duh. We already know who the killer is. We just gotta find her."

Zora held her hand up again, swatted the air. Zach flinched, hands up in protection mode.

"Don't make me hit you again."

"What? We know Mrs. Turlington didn't kill her husband!"

"We don't know any such thing. You can't even remember the night!"

He shrugged. "Seems pretty much like common sense."

"Something you don't have."

"So now what?"

"Guess we go pay Cleavon Smalls a visit. Mrs. Turlington said he had a real mad-on for the senator. Maybe he can lead us to your mystery bimbo."

"Not a bimbo."

"Make yourself useful for a change, Mr. Bimbo. Find out where Smalls's office is."

The Olathe Courthouse, located on the other side of town, meant they hit the road again.

Zora fumed behind the wheel as her minivan exhaust smoke cooked away. Any consoling words at this point would just instigate another head-slap. Zach considered taking the gun from her, but then tossed the notion away. Why give Zora any ideas?

Zora parked in front of the government office building, cursed at her seatbelt like a sailor and finally got out of the van.

Hitching up her pants, she said, "You're Smith. Detective John Smith."

"Kinda boring, sis."

"Too bad I can't make this more fun for you."

"Hey, no problem, Zor. I'll just roll with it."

She groaned, stormed off ahead of him.

Smalls's secretary sat in the center of the large waiting room, looking at them over her glasses. When Zach approached her desk, she gave her hair a come-hither shake and nibbled on the end of a pen. He was already in.

"Hello, I'm detective Laura Jones with the KCMO—"

"And what's your name, darling?"

A smile, EZ Brite style. "Shannon."

"Well, now, Shannon, that's a pretty name. Suits you well."

Zora glared at Zach, arms akimbo in a menacing gym teacher's pose.

"Thank you. How can I help you?"

She only had eyes for Zach, the eight month pregnant woman invisible to her.

"We need to see your boss, Alderman Smalls. Official police business, ma'am."

"I see...and may I ask what this is pertaining to?"

"We're investigating the murder of—"

"Would you please tell Alderman Smalls we're here?" said Zora. "Now?"

"And how 'bout when I come back, you give me your phone number, darlin'?"

"Hmm. And why would I do that? Maybe—"

"Oh for God's sake! Please tell him we're here! *Now!*"

Shannon gave Zora a prissy look, the type his sister used to get from the mean girls in school. With a voice as cool as shaved ice, Shannon spoke into her phone. "Mr. Smalls, there are two detectives here who—"

Behind them, a door cracked open. Alderman Cleavon Smalls came at them fast, nearly trotting, hand extended. Wearing a serious "call me Cleavon!" smile.

"Detectives! I wondered when you might talk to me!"

He moved with the odd grace big men carried well. Except for Burly Brian, of course. Smalls pumped Zach's hand, gave Zora a petite, polite, bare-minimum shake.

"Come in, come into my office!" He whirled, rolling back into his cubbyhole of an office. A big hand flourished over the two chairs across from his desk. He performed a little standing-in-place jig, closed the door for the finale. Every gesture he made looked podium-ready. Out of breath, he collapsed into his chair, mopping his head with a handkerchief. On his desk sat a tiny television dialed into the latest developments on Senator Turlington's murder, everyone's show of choice today. He grinned at them, happy as a lark. "A lovely day!"

"Um, yeah. I'm detective Laura Jones and this is—"

"Smith. John Smith."

"Heh. I like that...Smith and Jones." He sat back, tugging on a low-hanging earlobe (too much tugging, thought Zach), apparently pondering their names. He snapped back to the present, pointed at Zora. "If you don't mind my askin', ma'am, how long 'til your little voter drops?"

"Feels like any minute now."

He shook his head, worked up sad puppy eyes. "Why...that's just terrible. Simply terrible. I might have to have a word with the KCMO police superintendent, make sure you get full maternity leave."

"That's not necessary, Alderman—"

"Nonsense! I'm a firm believer in equality and women's rights! Vote for me, Cleavon Smalls. The only thing small about me's my name!" He leaned over his desk, waiting for applause. Zach stared at the TV, waiting for Smalls's political advertisement to end. "So…let's get started, Smith and Jones."

Zora pointed toward the TV. "As you well know, last night Senator Turlington was shot dead. We—"

"Terrible. Absolutely terrible." But his accompanying smile illustrated what he really thought. "Now…I've gotta say, it's not so terrible for me. Looks like I'm a lock now for the senate."

"Yes, I can see you're mourning."

"Hey, don't get me wrong. Hal was a real nasty piece of work, a real—pardon my French—son-of-a-bitch. Frankly I'd like to buy his killer a fancy steak dinner."

"I see…" said Zora. "Care to elaborate, Alderman?"

"The guy had no morals, no scruples. Anything he did—taking kickbacks, floating gimmicked city contracts—was to line his pockets. And the guy had the libido of a Kennedy, a blond in every pond, so to speak. Not like me, happily and faithfully married for thirty years! Cleavon Smalls, the only thing small about me—"

"Is your name. Got it. Did the senator have a special companion? Someone who he saw on a regular basis?"

"Now, that I can't help you with, ma'am. We didn't exactly run in the same social circles if you get what I mean." He favored Zach with a wink. Zach winked back, immediately felt uncomfortable doing so. Men probably shouldn't wink at one another. Not that Zach had anything to worry about, after all.

"So no one you know of."

"It is what it is." Smalls spread Zen-like hands.

"Uh-huh. Alderman, where were you last night between the hours of eleven and two in the morning?"

"Burning the midnight oil, of course! Right here in my office. And before you ask, I was alone, last man standing. Because I'm a dedicated servant to the people. Cleavon Smalls! The only thing small about me—"

"Surely there was someone who saw you coming or going."

His jowls got a wet-sounding workout when he shook his head. "Not a soul. It's lonely being a dedicated man in a not so dedicated business. I wish I could tell you I had an iron-clad alibi, have someone verify my whereabouts. I honestly do! But, like most nights, this is where I was. A believer in a solid work ethic and high moral standards." Big-time politician smile, hands offering up nothing. "I can definitely tell you I didn't kill the man if that sets your mind at ease."

"Not really."

"Hey, I might've despised the man, but I didn't kill him. I'm not a killer. I'm afraid you'll just have to take me at my word, and my word is good. As sure as my name is Cleavon Smalls, the only—"

"I wish it was that easy, Alderman. Taking you at your word. But…my faith in politicians only takes me so far."

His smile dropped, changing his entire demeanor. "Detective, I assure you I didn't kill the senator."

"Mm-hm. If you can think of anything at all that could help validate your story—"

"Not a story. I'm all about the truth. That's what Cleavon Smalls stands for."

"And Detective Laura Jones would like to stand for an honest-to-God alibi."

"Look…I don't know everything Hal was caught up in. Wish I could help you more. I just know he loved his prostitutes. It doesn't really even surprise me he was found dead in his…love nest."

"Not a love nest," muttered Zach.

The Alderman stared at him, then went back to preaching. "But I'm an honest man. Unlike Hal. Just ask around. I'm incapable of taking kickbacks, let alone murdering a man." He looked down at the TV, gave it a double-take.

He wasn't the only one. A sketch of Zach filled the screen. A crummy likeness, his eyes way too close together. Made him look stupid. But recognizable enough.

Smalls jacked a thumb to the screen. "See? There's your killer. White guy, full head of hair." He squinted at Zach, his mind clearly working to make the connection. "Not like me at all."

Zach averted his eyes, looked behind him through the window. Two men stood in the waiting room, talking to Shannon. Suits. Good, fitting ones. With seriously furrowed brows.

Crap.

"You're not helping me very much here, Alderman. You—"

"Um, Detective?"

"Give me something, Alderman, anything!"

The voices from the waiting room rose, heated.

"Hey, Detective?" Zach nudged her with an elbow.

"*What?*"

"I think…we're needed back at headquarters." He cocked his head toward the window. "Something's come up."

Zora sucked in a breath. "Okay, Alderman, that's all for now. We've gotta—"

"How about a business card? In case I think of anything else."

"Sorry. We're out."

And out of time.

The chair groaned when Smalls shot up. Both hands out. "Before you go, can you say it?"

"Say what?" Zora peeked out the window again. The two detectives were coming toward Small's office, Shannon yammering behind them.

"Don't leave town."

"Oh, for God's…Fine. Don't leave town."

Smalls clapped. "*Fantastic.* Remember, Detectives…vote for me, Cleavon Smalls. The only thing small—"

"Yeah, yeah, yeah." Zora reached for the doorknob. The door swung open. The two detectives (indistinguishable in their frat boy haircuts) narrowed their eyes in unison. Part of their training, no doubt.

"I'm sorry…excuse me." Zora shot past them. Zach hurried after her with his head down, but his likeness still plastered on the TV.

Crap, crap, crap! Move it, move it, move it!

The detectives entered Smalls's office. As soon as the door shut, it opened again. Zach felt four official eyes burrowing into his back. Shannon, wringing her hands, frowned as he blew by her. Disappointed, no doubt. But no time for fun.

Almost to the hallway, just a little bit to go…

"Detective?" called out Shannon.

"Yes?" Four voices answered.

Gah.

But Zach had to turn around, not in his nature to leave a lady in waiting. Standing in the office doorway, the detectives glared at him.

"I thought you wanted my phone number." Shannon looked at Zach, back to the detectives, again at Zach. Watching a tennis match.

With one hand on the exit door, Zora hunched her shoulders. She whispered, "Come on, Zach."

"Um, I'll call you later for it," Zach called to the receptionist. Then, under his breath, "go, go, *go*."

Zora pushed into the hallway. Smalls's voice rose from his office. Loud, the only way he knew how to talk.

"But they're detectives," shouted Smalls. "I'm telling you, as sure as my name is—"

"Stop! Wait!" The detectives yelling now.

Zora grabbed her brother's arm, hustled him toward the elevators. She pounded the button. Footsteps clomped over the hardwood floor from within the office area.

"Stop them!"

"Dammit! Come on!" Zora smacked the elevator panel one more time, hissed at its noncompliance. Then she broke into a run, her destination the steps at the end of the hallway. Zach followed, hearing a door open at his back.

Zora shoved the stairwell door open, clambered down the cement steps. A stampede of echoes filled the empty stairwell.

"Hurry, dammit, Zach!"

At the bottom of the stairs, fingers of daylight reached in. Zora smacked into the exit door, bounced off of it. Then pushed it open. She reached back in, pulled the fire alarm. The shrill alarm buzzed with the intensity of a dental drill.

"Why'd you do that?" asked Zach.

"To get more bodies in the cops' way! Shut up and run!"

People filed out of the building, a mass exodus. Zach thought he saw a gun rise above the crowd. One of the detectives trapped within the panicking people.

"Go! Don't stop. And quit looking back, Zach!"

Pregnant or not, Zora scrambled into the van in no time, a new record. Holding her breath and pale as chalk as she drove the minivan to freedom.

"Well…I think that went pretty good, huh?" said Zach.

Smack.

Chapter Seven

S till no closer to finding out the truth. Dammit." Zora pulled off the highway at 95th Street, parked the van in a shopping center lot.

"What're we doing? Shopping for new clothes?" Zach's eyes lit up, hopeful.

"No, we're not friggin' shopping. I'm thinking."

"What about Alderman Smalls? You think he had anything to do with it?"

"Doubt it. He was practically thrilled to death he didn't have an alibi, reveling in it."

"Yeah, that was a little weird."

"But guys like that? They're just excited to be involved in their own reality show with the law. Living out their fantasy. Something you know a thing or two about."

"This ain't no fantasy of mine, sis."

"Whatever you say, Hasselhoff."

"Guy sounds like a real jack-ass, though. Turlington I mean."

"Not the husband or politician of the year, that's for sure."

"Maybe Turlington crossed the wrong guy in his crooked deals. Smalls said he was up to his neck in crime."

"I don't know, I don't know, I don't *know*!" She winced, rubbed a circle out on her belly. "Damn baby's telling me it's time to eat. Fast-food burger."

"Um…can we get salads?"

Zora stared at her brother, shaming him into silence. "No, we're not getting *salads*. Or kale or anything like that."

As they entered the *Deep Belly Burger* drive-through lane, Zach remained quiet. Reverently so, almost. Zora needed the down-time, thrilled her brother'd learned one thing today.

"Squawk, rawk, gronk, sepsis?"

Zora leaned out the window, her ear close to the menu box, trying to decipher what the robot said. "Yeah, I didn't get a word of that. Just give me two burgers, cheese, the works. Large fries. Diet Coke."

"Sis, it's kinda pointless getting a Diet Coke with all that—"

She hushed him with a finger jabbed over her lips. No one gets between a pregnant woman and her culinary cravings. "What're you getting?"

"Um, nothing, I guess."

"Suit yourself." Back to the box, she said, "That's it."

Zora pulled up to the next window, greedily grabbed the grease-darkened sack. "Okay, I've got an idea...something I should've thought about before."

"What's that?"

"An old work acquaintance of mine. Miles."

"Yeah? What's he do?"

"If he's still at it—haven't talked to him in years—he writes a blog. A scandal piece about Kansas City. 'Kansas City Korruption.' He's big on alliteration. Guy loves him some conspiracy theories, loves to find fault in politicians. If anyone knows what Senator Turlington was up to, it's Miles. Maybe he can even suss out your mystery bimbo."

"She's not a...oh, whatever." Zach threw his hands up, knew when he was beat.

Back on the road, Zora spoke around the burger invading her mouth. "There're crayons and a pad of paper in the back seat. Get it."

"Um, why?"

"Just get it!" Zora embellished her latest bite with a small burp.

"Gross, sis."

"Yeah? You try eating for two. Then we'll talk gross. Do what I tell you."

Zach unsnapped his seat belt, leaned over the back seat, scrounging. With an elbow jab, Zora moved him over. "Get your stripper ass outta my face! Hello! Eating here!"

"Geeze, Zor, chill out. Okay, got it." He pulled out a purple crayon, ready, an enthused kindergartner.

"Draw a picture of the woman."

"What? I'm not a sketch artist!"

"Just do the best you can!"

"Okay…whatever." Zora had no doubt her brother's sketch would suck. But they needed something to go on, something visual to show Miles. Zach hunched over the pad, concentrating, suffering for his art. Sticking his tongue out from the corner of his mouth and squinting, He grunted, scratched through his work, flipped the page and started over. Picasso on the job.

Finally, he sat up and smiled at his drawing. "Yeah…yeah…that's her."

Zora snuck a glance at his portrait and nearly swerved into oncoming traffic. "Oh good Gawd, Zach! Samantha could draw better than that!"

"Hey! I told you I'm not a sketch artist." He studied it, nodded his head. "It's not all that bad. It looks like her."

"It looks like an egg on top of an hourglass! It took you that long to draw *that*?"

"I think I captured her. You know my memory still isn't what it should be."

"Never mind… That's *not* going to help."

"Whatever." Carefully, he folded the drawing, tucked it into his suit jacket. "Still think it looks like her."

"So, what, you're sleeping with Legos now?"

"I didn't sleep with her. And I *didn't* sleep with the senator!"

"Keep telling yourself that." Another mean shot. But a foul mood weighed Zora down. Mainly because she felt like a ripe watermelon, ready to split at the rind.

Compared with the nicer places in the KCMO metro area they'd been racing through today, Miles's neighborhood came in dead last. Even worse than Fireman Freddie's dump of an apartment complex. Miles lived on the top floor of a pseudo-renovated warehouse building. Zora wondered if halfway through the job, the architect realized the futility of the project and gave up. Even the brickwork had weathered, faded and crumbling. Bird droppings decorated the upper face, the only fresh adornment.

On a narrow street next to the building, Zora cut the engine. Next to Zach, a window shade suddenly snapped down.

"Nice neighborhood, sis. I think the rats vacated it a couple decades ago."

"Yeah, well…it's how Miles chooses to live. Tell you something, though, assuming Miles still lives here, I'm sure he's got a better security system than the Turlingtons. He's…a little paranoid. Be careful what you say to him. Hell, just let me do the talking. Our usual routine."

As they walked up wooden stairs, a door inched open on the second landing. And just as quickly shut. A single bulb swayed above them, shifting their shadows over the mildewed walls. Caused by a draft or someone having just fled? For security, just for old time's sake, Zora snapped open her purse, felt around for the pistol's butt. Gripped it and kept her hand glued to it. Something skittered by their feet. Zach jumped.

"Thought you were used to working with vermin, Zach," whispered Zora.

"Funny."

At the top floor, Zora knocked on a door, the only one in the hallway.

Music blasted out from the apartment. Loud and awful, death metal. Yep, Miles still lived in the 'hood.

Zora knocked again, louder. The music died. Soft thumps, a hasty yet hushed dance of feet. A small click. Metallic? A gun? Zora gulped. Miles's paranoia had skyrocketed.

Finally, "Who is it?" Harsh, abrupt, pissed off.

"Miles, hey, it's me, Zora. Zora LeFevre. Um…you probably remember me as Zora Caulfield. From back in the day? We worked together…I was at Denham and True Security?"

Silence. Then a succession of chains unthreading, locks turning, clamps unlatching. Secured by a chain lock, the door opened, just a crack. A bloodshot eyeball peeked out from behind unruly black bangs.

"Zora?"

"Yep. Hey, Miles, long time no—"

"*Who's* that with you?"

"He's just my brother, Miles. Harmless. He's…nothing but a, ah, stripper."

"Not a stripper, a male—"

She stepped on Zach's foot. "I need to talk to you, Miles."

"What about?"

"Senator Hal Turlington."

The door shut. Maybe Zora needed a secret password. The final chain slid back. Miles opened wide, using the door as a shield between him and his visitors. "Hurry up, hurry up. Get inside!"

As soon as they cleared the door, Miles slammed the door shut behind them. He completed his ritual, locking up Fort Knox.

Ratchet, clack, shgggg…

While Miles's paranoia had been amped up, his digs seemed to be stuck in a ten-year-old time loop. Void of any functionally comfortable furniture other than a tired sofa, the same green beast Zora'd sat on years ago, electronics lined the walls, filling every space. Computer screens provided a succession of green and white blinking Christmas lights. An overhead fluorescent bulb buzzed at them, an incessant fly. Oriental carpets overlaid the many windows.

Welcome to Miles's cavern.

Miles looked like he hadn't seen the sun in a decade. With skin white as Zach's teeth, his only color came from the dark crescents orbiting his eyes. His black hair hung down long, unruly, pony-tailed up in back. Getting his Howard Hughes recluse on, just not nearly as wealthy. The life of a dedicated conspiracy theorist.

"Hey, Miles, it's good to see you again." Zora stuck her hand out, quickly withdrew it, remembering Miles's germ phobia.

She hadn't warned Zach, though. He thrust his hand out, waiting. "Nice to meet you, Miles. I'm Zora's brother, Zach."

Miles stared at the offending hand, shuddered. "Why'd you bring a stripper here, Zora?"

Insulted, Zach yanked his hand back in. Kneaded it a little bit. "Hey, I'm a male dancer and I take offense to—"

Zora whacked the back of Zach's head. No need for covert moves here. For once, Zach didn't say another word. Some dogs are easier trained than others. "Miles, my brother's got himself into a bit of a jam. You're the only one who could possibly help. I mean, with your talents and all." The way to every eccentric genius's heart? Slobber 'em up with a heaping dosage of butt-kissing.

Bullseye! Miles softened, a smile exposing yellowed teeth, the by-product of a steady diet of junk food. Zora mentally noted to change her diet as soon as she pushed out her newest burden of joy. "Well…I enjoyed working with you in the past, Zora. Come on in, come on in! Have a seat. Wait!" Behind the sofa, Miles pulled out an industrial sized roll of plastic. Tore off a long strip and draped it over half of the sofa. "Okay…now you can sit."

Zora plopped down in the middle, Zach next to her. Her brother fidgeted on the plastic, rearranging himself, apparently unable to get comfortable.

Scrunch, rimple, shrak…

"Will you please sit still, Zach? I *swear*, worse than my kids."

Miles sat on the uncovered section of the sofa. "Okay, what's this about Turlington?"

"I'm sure you know about his murder." Miles nodded, brow brought low in journalistic integrity. "Well, my brother—"

"Wait." *Fsk, fsk.* Miles scratched at his unshaven face. "You're him. Oh my God, you're him!" He jerked a thumb back to a TV screen. "You're the male prostitute the cops are looking for in connection—"

"Okay, okay, I'm not a male prostitute. I'm a—"

"I knew Turlington was bad news! Knew it! But I had no idea he was gay! Totally blew me away! Not sure how that escaped me. I must be slip—"

Crunch, timple, scrunch…

"The senator wasn't gay! And I'm not—"

"Blew my mind! Zora, you know me, I don't like to report on salacious, sensationalistic personal details, but this…this!" Miles left earth for a bit, his eyes roving his inner galaxy.

Zora guided him back home. "Miles? Okay, Miles?"

"Hm?"

"Things aren't what they seem to be. Zach woke up this morning. Next to the dead senator. With no memory. Well...little memory. He was roofied. By a woman, a blonde."

"Really?" Miles patted down his pockets, came up empty-handed. Zora ripped out a sheet from her note-pad, handed it to him along with a pen. "Thanks. Okay...give me what you got." He started scribbling, fast and furious.

"Miles, I'll give you an exclusive on the story. But...I've gotta ask you to hold off publishing it. At least until we find out who killed Turlington. Deal?"

The journalist grimaced, sucked air in through his teeth. Wagged his head. "Fine. Start from the beginning..."

Zora filled him in, Zach interjecting on occasion, usually defending his sexual orientation. Zora wanted to gag him, tie him up in a corner.

"Wow...this is...wow..." Miles appeared exhilarated, tired eyes now at full moon. The scandal of a lifetime just made his day.

"Exactly. Now...I know you've been after Turlington for a while. I've read some of your exposes about his...questionable ethics in office." She hadn't really, just riding a hunch.

"Damn straight. He's bad news."

Bingo. "That's what I gather. Do you have any idea who might've wanted to kill the senator?"

"That's like asking if anyone wanted to kill Hitler!" Miles giggled. "Dude had enemies out the wazoo. But always came out smelling like a rose. Hell, I'm pretty sure he was mobbed up at one time, in bed with the local Kansas City mafia."

"Oh, really?"

"Yeah!" Now on the edge of his seat. "He kept tossing the mob city contracts like they were candy. Questions were raised—mostly by me, thank you very much—about the validity of these contracts. And plenty of funds went missing. And I know where those funds went, too! Zora...do you think this was a mob hit?"

Zora thought about it, weighed her answer carefully. "No. I really don't think so. It doesn't seem very...mobby since there was a mystery woman involved. And she went to great lengths to drag Zach into her plan."

"Oh." Miles's shoulders sank. Maybe not so much the expose of a lifetime, after all.

"But, don't worry, Miles…this is still gonna be a good scandal, one worthy of your award-winning blog."

"You think?"

"I do. Now, you said you know where Turlington's misappropriated funds ended up. Where?"

"Well…he had a mistress. Pretty much a kept woman. Bought her a nice house, gave her a car…hired her a driver even."

"A Cadillac, Miles?"

"Yeah…yeah, I think so."

Srrrppp, scrunch, tmple, tump…

Zach joined Miles on the edge of the sofa. "Wait! Is this…" Zach reached into his pocket, whipped out his earlier drawing with a soap opera's worth of melodrama. "…her?" Zora imagined Zach heard a musical sting in his head, time for commercial break!

Miles squinted at the drawing. "Wait…is that an egg?"

"It's not an egg. It's her!"

"Looks like an egg on top of a river or—"

"That's not a river! It's her body!"

Miles scratched an ear, clicked up a corner of his mouth. "It's not a very good drawing. Kinda looks like something a kid would—"

"I'm not a sketch artist!"

Crunch, timple, tumple…

"Yeah, but really, it doesn't even look like a person. It's just all—"

"Okay, Miles. Yeah, the picture sucks." Zora gave Zach a look, shook her head. "But do you have a name for Turlington's mistress?"

"Sure do. I can do you one better. Got an address." Miles shot up, sat down in front of one his work-stations. His fingers ripped across the keyboard. "Selena Darkly's the name I have. Kinda doubt it's her real name, though. I dunno, sounds kinda strippery or—"

"Nothing wrong with stripper names!"

"Shut up, Zach."

Miles hit the return button again. Sat back with a satisfied smile. "That her?" A driver's license image. Selena Darkly. Blond. A smile that didn't budge her cheeks. Crows feet planted at the corners of her eyes. Definitely work done. Aged thirty-six and Zora suspected that was another lie. Ms. Selena Darkly appeared very comfortable with lies.

A shocked look on his face, Zach clutched the back of Mile's computer chair. "That's her. I remember…definitely Cat."

"Definitely *not* 'Cat'! But it's our girl." Zora scribbled down the address. "Miles, you've been a great help. Thanks much, my friend."

"Anytime. Just don't forget to call me." He pantomimed using a phone. "Let me know the rest of the details and when I can punch the publish button."

"Will do. Let's go, Zach."

Again, Zach offered his hand.

Miles said, "Dude, I'm *not* gonna touch that. I don't know where it's been!"

"Ain't that the livin' truth," said Zora.

In the hallway, Zach said, "Zor, this is the best news we've had all day."

"Don't get your hopes up yet, brother. But, yeah…it might be our first break." She smiled, letting her brother bask in a bit of victory. Even if it might be a bit premature. Zora'd learned the hard way, it ain't over 'til the bad guys are in jail.

"Weird friends you got, though."

"Oh, really? Says the guy who's sleeping with plastic old ladies and letting their chauffer watch."

"Uncool! I *didn't* sleep with her. And the driver *didn't* watch… I think."

"'You think'…whatever…you can't even remember, let alone think."

Outside, dusk had fallen, painting the neighborhood an even deeper shade of danger. A car sat parked behind Zora's minivan. Very close, bumper to bumper close. A black Caddy.

Behind them, a fallen leaf snapped on the sidewalk. Zora turned, her hand grasping for the gun in her purse.

Tall, gruesome and silver materialized out of the building's shadows. His hand snagged Zora's wrist. Wrenched her purse away. Grinned as he commandeered her pistol. "Ah, ah, ah…let's play nice now."

Zach ran at the chauffer, growling. Dennis tossed the purse at Zora, freeing one of his hands.

He stepped back, lifted the gun. Steadied it. Closed one eye and aimed the gun at Zach.

Click.

A click Zora'd been on the receiving end of more than once, one she didn't particularly care for. And one that meant they couldn't overpower the driver.

Zach stood in place, bouncing. Fists lifted and curled up.

"Don't, Zach. Stop. You can't beat a bullet."

Zach lowered his fists, but kept shuffling his feet.

"That's a sensible girl," said Dennis. He jutted out a chiseled chin toward Zach. "Maybe your idiot brother should take a clue from you."

"I'm not an idiot…"

"Now, I'm sick and tired of chasing your asses all over Kansas City. Caught up with you at the courthouse, been following you ever since. You're coming with me now. No more bullshit!"

Zora righted her purse, strapped it over her shoulder, and said, "So…you gonna kill us now?"

Another grin. A not very comforting shrug. "I'm taking you to see Ms. Darkly."

"That's what you want? Well, hell…" Zora walked toward the Caddy, rapped her knuckles on the roof. "That's where we're going, too. Save me some gas money. Go on…take us to your leader."

Clearly confused about who to plug first, Dennis swung the gun between the siblings. "Fine. Here, pretty boy." He tossed his car keys toward Zach. "You're driving."

"Cool! Always wanted to get behind the wheels of a Caddy."

The chauffer settled the gun on Zora. "You! Big Momma…in the back seat with me."

Okay, now he's pissed me off.

100

Huffing, Zora fell into the back seat. Trying not to go all ninja on the bad guy's ass.

He called me Big Momma! No one talks to a pregnant woman that way. Gun or not.

Head lowered, Dennis slid in next to her. Still unable to sit up straight because of his height. Zora smiled, imagining him driving with his head stuck up through the sun-roof.

"Okay, pretty boy, take us to 35-South. Then go to—"

"We have the address," said Zora. "We know where we're going."

"Good. Then everyone shut up and let's go. Don't try anything or I'll put a hole in you." The way he said it, Zora didn't doubt it. He marveled over the gun, admiring it with a greedy smile, anxious to put it to use.

Zach edged out into traffic. Singing. The damned EZ Brite theme song.

"Quiet," ordered the chauffer.

"So…tell me, Dennis…is that your real name, Dennis?" asked Zora. "What do you and your boss lady intend on doing to us?"

"Not for me to say."

"How long've you been saddled up with Ms. Darkly? She pay good money? To, you know, kill people and stuff?" Part nerves, part strategy to put the thug off-guard, Zora couldn't shut up even if she wanted to. "Is that part of a chauffer's job these days? 'Must have good driving skills, silver hair, look like a German weight-lifter. Murderous intent a plus!'"

"Shut up."

"Really…I mean, are good driving jobs so hard to find these days, Dennis?"

"I said, shut up!" The gun tapped Zora's belly. Another thing she'd make the chauffer regret. "Don't make me tell you again! I want it quiet!"

Zora had lots more she wanted to say. But you didn't argue at the end of a gun barrel.

Thirty minutes later, after a few quietly stated directions from Dennis, they arrived at their destination. Zora hoped it wouldn't be their final destination.

Turlington had ponied up some serious cash for his mistress's digs. Nestled out in the woods of the southernmost part of Kansas City, the house loomed large, three stories' worth. Skeletons of other houses had gone up in the distance, not yet inhabited. Completely isolated. Perfect for a senator's secret love nest. And a perfect killing grounds.

Zach turned off the ignition. "Now what?"

"Give me the keys." Dennis caught the tossed keys, shoved them into his pocket. "Now get out. Don't try anything. Or Big Momma and her baby gets it."

Strike three, he's out!

"Please don't shoot her," said Zach as he scooted out, hands in the air.

"Well, what're you waiting for? Get out." Another gun gesture. Big man with a weapon.

Zora dug into her purse. Hummed a bit.

"What're you doing now?"

"A woman's gotta look her best when she calls on a stranger. Particularly one who wants to kill her."

Dennis hesitated, obviously perplexed by the world of cosmetics. "Just make it fast."

Stupid. So stupid. It's almost too easy.

Her hand in her purse, Zora gripped the vial. Flipped the cap off.

"Oh, one more thing, Dennis…"

Dennis sighed, a thug of few words.

"Never, ever, *ever* call me 'Big Momma' again!" She dropped the purse the same time the pepper spray came up.

Tsssssss…

A nice, long dose to the eyes.

Dennis screamed. Not having a good day. His hands went up, so did the gun.

Crack.

Runch.

A bullet punctured the roof. Smoke rose from the barrel. While the chauffer writhed in agony, Zora grabbed the gun.

Zach hunched over by her door, panic in his eyes. "Sis! You okay!"

"Better than Dennis." She gave him an extra squirt, one to remember her by. Zach helped her out. She leaned back in, said, "Dennis, I hope you've learned your lesson. Treat pregnant women with respect. Everyone has a mother. I suspect even you. Unless you were created in a laboratory…which isn't such a far-fetched idea the more I think about it."

Damn, this feels great! Too bad baby on board doesn't agree.

"What're you laughing at, Zor?" Zach held onto her, rushing her away from the car. Like she needed help, a fragile pregnant woman.

"Get your hands *off* me. Fully capable woman here."

"*Pregnant* woman."

"Don't even go there with me, Zach! Now, come on…we gotta hurry. I'm sure your hooker heard the gunshot and is waiting for us."

Dennis was still shrieking, rocking the Caddy on its tires. But now he was winding down into a child's calming moan. They didn't have long.

On the doorstep, Zora held the gun high and hoped like hell she wouldn't have to try and shoot the lock off the door. Or God forbid, kick it open. The doorknob twisted easily in her hand, though. Quietly, the door swung open. It felt wrong, the door being unlocked. The trusting faith of country living or a trap?

"Sis, we can't just…go in the house," Zach whispered.

"Really, Zach? Really? All the other crimes we've committed today, a little B&E isn't gonna hurt us."

He looked puzzled, trying to work out what the letters stood for.

"Come on. Let's go."

Gun cocked and ready, Zora lead them inside. Bright lights emanated from every room. Ms. Darkly didn't live up to her name.

They tiptoed through the foyer, down a hallway. Into a large living room. Ms. Darkly sat on a love-seat, a posed statue, one leg crossed over the other. Unmoving. Except for the gun in her hand. That she gave a little wiggle to.

"Well, come on in then," she said. "Gun against gun. Are you going to risk it, Ms. LeFevre?"

"Willing to gamble if you are."

"I'm positive I can take out one of you, maybe both."

"Let's bet."

"Um, sis—"

"Or...I lower my gun. You lower yours," said Darkly.

"Ladies first."

Darkly smiled. Tried to at least. Maybe it was a grimace, Zora couldn't be sure, not with all of the woman's emotion-obscuring plastic work. The gun loosened in Darkly's grip, swung around a dainty finger. Then she placed it in her lap. "There. Friends now?"

Zora lowered her weapon. Tried to tuck it into her waistline. No going, not with baby occupying most of the space. She kept it down by her hip, ready to use it with a finger on the trigger. "Hardly friends. Why don't you tell me why you killed the senator? Why you tried to frame my brother?"

Long lashes flipped up. Darkly's mouth formed a puzzled "oh." "Why, Ms. LeFevre...that's what I wanted to ask you! Why your brother killed the late, not-so-great, Senator Turlington."

"I'm right here, you know," said Zach. "And I didn't kill—"

"Quiet, Zach! What're you talking about, Darkly?"

"Oh, my. It seems like we have quite a bit to catch up on. Please...be seated." She unleashed a waving roll of her hand toward a sofa. At least it didn't have plastic on it like Miles's furniture. Zora figured Darkly used up her plastic allowance on her face.

Zora sat, Zach reluctantly so.

"Now...where's Dennis? What have you done to him this time?" Darkly looked out into the hallway, squinting through awning length lashes.

"I'm sure he'll be along shortly. I just gave him a little incentive to stop insulting me."

"I see...you really need to stop doing things to my driver. You've wrecked my car—"

"He wrecked it."

"...you hit him with baby excrement, knocked him out, flattened my tire...and now this?"

"Cry me a river, lady! What about everything *you've* done?"

She cawed at the ceiling. "Me? Fine. Let's start over…I'm Selena Darkly." Her hand went out, waiting for them to kiss it or something. Zach and Zora stayed put.

"Doubtful that's even your name, lady."

"Not important right now."

"How about you start by telling us what *is* important? Before I perforate your pretty, plastic face."

She frowned, her cheekbones staying high. "So hurtful. Very well then…I had an affair with Hal."

"Shocker."

"Ms. LeFevre, I'm trying my best to be civil. I would expect you to show me the same courtesy."

"Yeah, 'cause murder and slipping people roofies is so very civil."

"Regardless…our affair went on for quite some time. Hal was good to me, bought me this house, hired Dennis for me. But…a few weeks ago, he said he was ending our relationship. That he'd found a younger girl." She dabbed at crocodile tears. "Said he was going to take back the house…like I never meant anything to him."

Yeah, because a fancy house for a slutty mistress is what love's all about.

"Too bad, so sad, Darkly. Still no reason to kill the guy."

"But I didn't! Honestly…we thought Zach did."

"Again, not a killer. Not even gay or a—"

"How 'bout you tell me what happened after the senator showed up to your sleazy hotel room?"

"Well, Zach, the dear boy…" Darkly gave him a warm smile. Zora couldn't believe he returned it. "…he'd apparently had too much to drink. And he passed out."

"Not true."

"A difference in perspective. I'd called Hal earlier, told him to meet me at the room downtown. That I had something important to tell him, something that couldn't wait. And since Zach…the dear boy…was passed out, I thought I'd take advantage of the situation. I had Dennis drug Hal. Drag him into bed next to Zach."

"Ah, I think you have it wrong, Selena," offered Zach. "I think you might've accidentally, I dunno, roofied me or something?"

"No, Zach...we *know* she did," said Zora. "What happened next, Darkly?"

"Dennis took me home, leaving the two sleeping beauties slumbering away. Then I called several reporters. The police. Anonymously, of course."

"Of course," said Zora, proudly riding a sneer. "And that's it?"

"That's it. Next thing I know the media's all abuzz about Hal's...tragic death. So, Zach...tell me..." She leaned forward, fingertips poised on her crossed legs. Showing them off to elicit a confession out of Zora's brother. Knowing him, Zora thought he might fall for it, too. "Why did you kill the senator?"

"I didn't, dammit!"

The front door banged open. Loud footsteps thundered down the hall. Dennis stood, breathing hard, sweatier than a politician at a hearing. "Ms. Darkly, you want me to take out the trash?" Through red eyes, he glared at Zora.

Selena swatted a hand. "No, not yet, Dennis. I don't have what I want yet."

And I bet that's all she ever gets. What she wants.

"Just stay right there for now. You'll know when I need you."

"Ma'am." Dennis tipped his head her direction.

"Well, Zach," continued Darkly, "if you didn't kill Hal...who did?"

"That's what we'd like to know." Zora tried to stand, couldn't quite make it. The baby tugged her back into the upholstery. She tried to cover up her setback by speaking faster. "Let's just say you're telling the truth—which I kinda think you're not cause everything out of your mouth is as phony as your face—" Darkly's lips actually moved, wrinkling together at Zora's insult. "Let's say you drugged my brother, had it in your mind all along to do so. To put the senator into a bind, one he couldn't get out of. Framed in a gay love nest."

Zach sighed, but for once didn't defend his so-called honor.

"For now, let's just go with that," continued Zora. "But why didn't you just come forward with the truth? Talk to the media about your sordid little tryst. That would've been enough to ruin the senator's political ambitions. Not to mention his marriage. And his affair with his newer, younger, *improved* model. Why the elaborate gay frame-up?"

"Because I'm not that kind of girl, Ms. LeFevre!"

"Ah, correction...not a girl at all. More like a woman who—"

"Let's not get nasty. I have a reputation to uphold, after all. A career that's just starting to take off. It—"

"What? As a porn star?"

"Hardly." She hissed, poisonous as a snake. "But you have the latter part right. I'm an up and coming actress. Hal set me up with a few of the right people. He—"

"Oh. You been in anything I might've seen, ma'am?" Zach sat up, no longer appearing bored.

"Maybe you've seen me in *The Scattering, Part 3*? No? Perhaps you saw me in—"

"For God's sake, Zach! You want her autograph, too?"

He shrugged. "Depends on what she's been in, I guess."

"You're cute, Zach." Darkly leaned back, raised her crossed leg a little higher. Absolutely no shame. "I knew there was a reason I picked you."

Zach smiled. Just too much for Zora. With a one-two-three roll of her arms, she levied herself out of the sofa. "Get a room, why don't you, Zach? No, wait! You already did! And look how *that* turned out!"

With a hangdog look, Zach blended in with the sofa. "Oh, yeah."

"I swear!" Zora paced the room, getting into full-on detective mode. "Darkly, you just admitted you 'picked' Zach. He was a part of your plan all along. You roofied him."

Darkly gave her head a little tilt. Shared a small smile, big on smarminess. And said nothing.

"So, Darkly...when you left the hotel room, did you lock it behind you?"

"No, of course not. I wanted the police, the media, everyone to see Hal in all his glory."

"Even if what you're saying is true—and again, you haven't exactly proven yourself high on the trustworthy scale—why'd you kill your detective? Martin?"

Selena's crossed leg lifted. Her foot tromped down on the floor like a horse's hoof. "Detective? *What* detective?"

Zora thought she looked, sounded, absolutely surprised. And she knew Darkly couldn't be that good of an actress.

"You didn't hire a detective?"

"No. Why in Heaven's name would I do that? To implicate myself?" Another guffaw aimed at the ceiling.

Then who in hell hired Martin? Who killed him?

"You didn't kill him?"

"We're not killers, Ms. LeFevre." She included Dennis in her game show hostess wave.

"No, just abductors, conspirators, exploiters, druggers—is that a word?—flesh-peddlers...am I leaving anything off your list? Never mind!" Zora paced, arms behind her back. Quite a stretch in her condition. "The phone."

"Excuse me?"

"Zach's phone. Did you take it?"

"Of course not. I'm not a thief after—"

"Yeah, I know what you are, Darkly. Where was the phone when you left the hotel room?"

"Not sure. I took it away from Zach after I saw he was recording his cute song. Didn't want anything incriminating on it, after all."

"I left it by the bed, ma'am," said Dennis.

"If this is true...the killer took the phone...hired the detective...then killed him."

"Whatever you say, Ms. LeFevre. Frankly, I don't understand what you're even talking about now."

That makes two of us. I'm not even gonna count Zach.

"What are we doing here, Darkly? Why'd you have Godzilla over there kidnap us?"

"I wanted to find out why Zach did poor Hal in." She batted goo-goo eyes his way. "And to have Dennis take him down to the police station with his confession." Her hand slipped under her dress. Zach's eyes widened. She slipped out a phone from a garter belt riding high on her thigh, everything about her trampy. "But you're playing hard to get. Guess we'll let the police do their own work. Pity. I'd hoped to have my name kept out of this. But no one can prove I drugged dear Zach, so I'm not worried. And as you said, Ms. LeFevre...maybe a little publicity wouldn't hurt my career after all. Dennis? Go to work." She shooed him on, went back to playing with her phone.

Dennis hunkered into a gorilla stance, arms and legs spread. Clopping his way toward Zach. Zach shot up from the sofa, arms rolling. Warming up. Dancing. Dennis swung a fist. Zach bobbed back, out of arm's range. Then Zach darted in, speed his weapon, clopped the chauffer's chin with a punch. The chauffer crashed back against the wall, but remained upright. Zach dove in again, staying low, adjusting for the height difference. A double punch to Dennis's belly. Jack-hammering, not letting up. Zora'd never admit it to her brother, but his stripper skills finally proved useful for something. Always the show-off, Zach twirled, jacked a foot up. Landed it onto Dennis's nose. Dazed, Dennis slipped down the wall, holding his nose. Moaning. *Really* a bad day for the guy.

Darkly watched the scuffle calmly, almost disinterested. High faith in her chauffer's strength. But she lifted the gun from her lap, a backup plan. Too bad for her she didn't notice Zora scoot up beside her.

Zora brought her gun-butt down on Darkly's head, hard enough to make the blond drop her gun. Quickly, Zora snatched the fallen gun. "Can't have you playing with toys. Liable to shoot your face off."

Darkly shook her head, suddenly very tired looking. "This is all pointless, you know. Ms. LeFevre…they're going to catch you soon. In fact, concerned citizen that I am, I just might call them myself."

"You really *suck* at making new friends!" This time Zora brought the gun-butt into Darkly's face. A couple times. A little too hard, knocked her out cold. Too bad. Zora kinda wanted to inflict more torture.

Still shuffling on his feet, fists up, Zach said, "You rock, sis!"

"And now we gotta roll." She collected Darkly's phone and joined her brother, looking down at the laid-out chauffer. "Dennis…Dennis, pay attention now. Please give me your car keys."

"You broke my noth! I'm not givin' you—"

"Dennis, don't make me bring out the enforcer again." The pepper spray frightened Dennis more than the gun. Just like all men, for some reason. So stupid, such wimps when it comes to pain.

Dennis shuddered, scooted sideways, reached into his pocket. The keys jangled in his shaking hand.

"Thanks Dennis. Ta-ta for now." She gave him a pat on the head, almost feeling sorry for him. Then scooted her brother the hell out of there.

Chapter Eight

Z ora demanded Zach drive, not that you had to tell him twice. The Caddy felt good, a true prestigious ride. If only his friends could see him, especially that damn Fireman Freddie.

"Who you calling now?"

"Phillip. Shh.... Hey honey... No, not yet. I know, I know... I'll explain when I get home.... When? Not sure. Soon, I hope." Zora grimaced, caught her breath. Something big brewing. "Oh, um, do you think you can arrange a ride to go pick up the minivan?... It's, ah, downtown at... Look, I'm not too happy about it either!... It's just something important I had to... Yes... Yes, he's still with me.... Don't *even* start. No, don't you start with me, Phillip!... The longer you keep me on the phone, the longer it'll take me to get home!... Yes... Enjoy your damn meat loaf! Love you, too!"

Not a whole lotta love evident in the way she shouted that last part, though.

"Phillip having a bad day?" Frankly, Zach didn't think he had any other kind. Guy should get out more.

"Shut up, Zach."

"Um, where we going?"

"For now, just far away from your girlfriend's house."

"She's not my girlfriend."

"Really? Hard to tell by the way you were making goo-goo eyes over her."

"Hey, she's a looker, what can I say?"

"Get your eyes checked. And have you forgotten she roofied you?"

"Well, I guess there is that."

"And the little part about how she kidnapped you. And set you up to look like Senator Turlington's gay lover."

And then there's that. I could maybe overlook the other things. Just not the whole gay framing thing.

"Zor, I'm kinda just driving around, you know. On auto-pilot."

"Your usual mode of operation."

"Do you think Selena did it? Killed Turlington?"

"Doubtful. She seemed actually surprised. I bet her acting's not that good in *The Scattering Part 3* or whatever."

"Huh. Did you get anything useful? Other than stealing a car?"

"I dunno. Maybe. Apparently Darkly never had your phone. Or so she says. And she claims she didn't hire the detective. There's someone else involved, someone we're overlooking. It's usually the most obvious person."

"Well, she said Turlington started a new affair with some young hottie. How 'bout her?"

"Who knows?" Zora's hands flapped up. "Everyone else seems to have agendas, political or sexual. Could be anyone."

"Yeah...you know...if I woke up next to a dead girl, we probably wouldn't be in this mess. So...sorry I got you involved."

"Gah. You're telling me you would've called the cops if your corpse pal was female?"

"Well...yeah. Duh."

Smack.

"Dammit! Not while I'm driving, okay?"

"Honestly, Zach, I swear...it's almost as if you care more about proving you're not gay than proving your innocence."

He had to think about that long and hard. A toss-up, really. Both options sucked.

"Well...I'm not gay."

"So you keep saying already! Maybe you protest too much?"

"The hell's that supposed to mean?"

"Think about it. Now, shut up. I'm trying to think."

Cautiously, fearing another head-slap, Zach snuck a glance at his sister. With closed eyes and a wrinkled forehead, she looked in pain. Probably her giving birth look. Still, he had to say it. The way their relationship rolled. Both of them always had to get the last word in. Hedging his bets, he said it fast. "I'm not gay. Really, I'm not."

Her eyes snapped open. "Wait! Say that again!"

"What? I've been saying it all along. And you know it's true. I'm not gay. Duh."

"Crap. Oh, crap. So dumb of me." She turned to face him, quite a chore. "Zach, when did that sketch of you first go up on TV?"

"Um...I don't know...maybe when we were at that politician's—what's his name's—office? I guess?"

"Let me verify that." Excited, she searched through her phone, tapped a few buttons.

"Sis? Who you calling?"

"Quiet. Miles, it's me, Zora! Pick up the phone, it's important!" She cupped a hand over the phone, stage-whispered, "He never picks up until he knows who it is. Miles! Hey! No, not yet...but soon, I hope. Got a question for you. You've been monitoring the Turlington murder all day, right? Good man... When did the reporters first mention Turlington had slept with a man?"

"I didn't sleep with—"

"Shh! No, not you, Miles. Sorry. And when did my brother's sketch first make the rounds? Uh-huh... You sure about that?... No, I didn't mean to question your complete mastery over the facts... Of course I know you're a consummate professional..." She quacked her hand, rolled her eyes. "That's what I need to know. Thanks, Miles, you're a gem."

She slapped the phone shut with more force than she'd used all day on Zach's head. "I know who the killer is, Zach."

"What?" Instinctively, his foot chunked down on the brake. They turned into a skid, slowed.

Stopped. A car passed them, honking. "Who? How?"

"Okay, Miles said your sketch wasn't released to the local news until mid-afternoon, around two or so."

"So?"

"And nothing was mentioned about Turlington's possibly being gay until around the same time. Not a *single* word."

"I'm still not following."

"I know you're not. Get us out of the middle of the road. *Drive.*" She pointed toward the windshield. Smiling for a change. A good look on her. "Think, Zach. Who did we talk to this morning? Before the whole gay debacle came to light?"

"Not gay."

"*Who?*"

He tugged a lip, remembering. "Crap. Mrs. Turlington!"

"Gold star for my brother!"

"But I don't know—"

"She said, 'My husband was out sticking it to some whore. Or *man.*'"

"Oh..."

"Yep. Not once did she mention she suspected he was gay, bi, whatever. And the media hadn't wrapped their hands around that fact yet."

"Um, *not* a fact—"

"Focus. Why would Mrs. Turlington bring up her husband's sleeping with a man? Unless she *knew* what happened. About your involvement."

"But maybe...he *was* sleeping with men. You know, as well as women."

"You're not building a good case for yourself, Zach!" She held a hand up, lowered her weapon. In too good a mood. "Let's go end this. Now."

"To Turlington mansion, Robin?"

"Ah, no. I'm Batman. You're Robin."

"But...Robin always wears those kinda gay, green trunks."

"Oh my God..."

Zora pulled out her gun, opened the chamber, peered inside. Apparently liked what she saw.

Grinning, she aimed the gun out the passenger window, faked a recoil. Whispered, "pow."

Zach considered everything, went over the day, all the interviews, the suspects.

And just like Zora's gun, his mind's chamber opened...

———————————

Something rustled in the darkness. Voices, underwater and garbled. No, his mind drowning. He tried opening his eyes, stubborn as ancient shades. Light trickled in, liquid and stinging. Blurry. Two figures surrounded him, looking down on him. A man and woman. Cat and her driver? No. Maybe. Think about it later. Eyelids so weighty, meaty. Just five more minutes...

Phht, phht, phht...

Someone having gas? No, too machine gun like, rapid-fire. *A gun?* Why would there be a gun in the hotel room? And, duh, it seemed too quiet for a gun.

Forcing his eyes open, he peeked. Just a crack.

An old woman. A guy in a suit. Holding a gun. Long barrel on it, kinda like what hit men used in movies. *A silencer?*

"Take the gun and the stripper's phone with you. Don't leave anything behind." A woman's voice, sorta broken. Or maybe the cracks in his head were leaking his brains out, making her voice sound that way.

Where the hell'd Cat get off to? Never did have our fun. Maybe we did, I dunno.

"Anything else?" The man speaking now. So boring. So lulling.

"That'll do nicely, Tufty." The woman's voice turned soft, speaking in baby talk. Tucking me into bed, her voice a lullaby. "Don't they just look so sweet together?"

"Yes, ma'am, they do, indeed."

"Let's go. Goodbye, Hal."

The door opened, closed. So did Zach's eyes.

But something didn't seem right.

Whatever. Time to worry about it later. Once he woke up from this dream. Weirdest damn dream ever.

EZ Brite, EZ Brite, totally toothy wonderful delight...

_____

"...you're right, Zor. Mrs. Turlington did it. So did Tufts, Turlington's advisor."

"What? *Now* you remember? *Now?* After everything we've been through?"

"Guess that's the way I roll."

"Yeah, well, let's hope your head doesn't roll on the guillotine."

He gulped. Envisioning the image. "Um, they don't still use the guillo—"

"Dammit. I should've seen this earlier. I'm off my game, Zach. Too long outta the field."

"Don't eat yourself up over it, sis. Could happen to anyone." He smiled, showed her his EZ Brite enhanced teeth. Irresistible, of course. To everyone but his sister.

"Something seemed off about the whole Mrs. Turlington and Tufts thing. I knew it, just knew it!"

"Think they're having an affair?"

"Probably. Everyone else wrapped up in this sordid mess is."

At the top of Mrs. Turlington's street, Zora shouted, "Stop!"

"What? Why?"

"It's time to go covert."

Zora said it like she enjoyed the idea. But Zach didn't know if his sister was up for it. "But it's quite a walk for...um..." He looked at her belly, back into her eyes.

"Good God, after everything else we've been through today, you're gonna start in on that? Piece of cake. Let's go. I'll show you how I roll."

As soon as they left the minivan, Zach ran from tree to tree, hiding in the shadows. Waiting for Zora to catch up. Gun in hand, she strolled down the middle of the street, master of the parade. Slaying a serious eye-roll.

"Honestly, Zach, when I said 'covert,' I didn't mean for you to skulk around like a serial killer. I just didn't want them to see the car's headlights. Ready? Or you wanna keep playing secret agent?"

Zach followed her to the door. Zora dropped her gun to her side, palming it as best she could. Rang the doorbell.

"This is covert?"

"Quiet. We've got surprise in our favor. Shock and awe. And I'm gonna shock the awe outta them."

Tufts face appeared in a side window. The door opened. Impassive as usual, he stared at them. Holding a hand behind his back.

"Yes? Detectives?" A purr affected his voice, a cat toying with mice.

"Just a few last questions, Mr. Tufts."

"No."

"Excuse me?"

"No."

"I'm sorry we can't accept that. Police business." Zora pushed the door open. Tufts, a blur of gray suit and pale flesh, spun behind her. He grabbed her with an arm around her throat. A gun to her temple.

"For God's sake," sputtered Zora, "does *everyone* have a gun?"

"It's Kansas." Tufts shrugged. Displayed his first smile, maybe ever.

"Now. I *know* you're not detectives. You're impersonating the law. Breaking into Mrs. Turlington's house. I'm well within my legal rights to shoot you. And that's what I'm going to do."

"Kick his ass, Zach!" Zora stomped on Tuft's foot, knocked his gun arm down. His finger squeezed the trigger.

Crack.

The bullet landed in Tuft's foot. He fell back to the floor, eyes closed, mouth open in a silent scream. Zora hopped away, turned, gun up. Zach dropped on top of Tufts. Tufts held the gun above his head as Zach reached for it.

"Move, Zach, I can't shoot him with you on top of him!"

Stronger than he looked, Tufts held onto the gun. Zach bashed the smaller man's gun hand onto the marble floor, reflexively squeezing off a series of bullets.

Bang, crack, zing...

Down the hallway, a marble bust exploded. Grey shrapnel rained down.

Pink, dink...

Zach slammed Tuft's hand onto the floor again. The gun spun away, a metallic swirl. Zora ran for it. Bent to pick it up. Couldn't quite make it. One hand on the wall, she lowered to one knee, retrieved the weapon, and stashed it into her purse.

Zach rolled across the floor with Tufts, trading positions. "I got this, sis! Go! Get Mrs. Turlington!"

"You sure?"

"He's got a bullet in his... *ugh*...foot. I can take him. Go!"

"I will...as soon as I can get up." Zora grabbed a drape, hoisted herself up. "Make him hurt, Zach." She raced down the hall to the stairwell.

Tufts rolled again, forcing Zach beneath him. He sat astride Zach, his hands squeezing Zach's throat. "Kill you...I'll... *kill* you!"

Zach brought his fist up into Tuft's exposed throat. *Fair play.*

Tufts flew back, his head smacking the floor with a sickly wet sound.

Zach rolled away, sprang to his feet. Dancing and bobbing, doing his thing. Fists ready, a foot prepped to launch.

Tufts surprised Zach. Up fast, spreading his weight evenly on planted legs, ignoring the bullet in his foot. "Come on," Tufts said. "Think you can take me? Let's see what you've got." He opened his hands, extending his fingers. Did some kinda twirling motion.

Crap. One of those karate guys.

On the balls of his feet, Zach danced closer. Two steps in, one back. Getting acquainted with his dance partner. Tufts spun, his foot coming up.

Tump.

Stunned by the blow to his face, Zach twisted, fighting for balance. Like a cat, he landed gracefully. A dizzy cat. Tufts roared, charged him.

Crik, chok!

Two rapid-fire punches, one to Zach's chin, the other just above his eye. Zach rolled with the blows, struggling to stay on his feet. Then backed up until the room quit spinning.

With a smile, Tufts ran at Zach again, head down like a rhino. Zach side-stepped, watched him fly by. Practically by instinct, Zach grabbed the marble pillar next to him. Timed it beautifully. As Tufts hurtled back, Zach spun on the pillar. Lifted both his legs. His super dance pole move, one for the ladies.

Smack.

Tufts went down. Stayed down.

Zach dropped from the pillar onto shaky legs. Kissed his fingers and held them up.

Thanks, Big Guy in the sky for my male dancing excellence.

Clapped his hands, wiped away imaginary dust. And had an epiphany.

No, dammit, I'm a stripper. And proud of it.

The tilt-a-whirl wouldn't stop, though. His knees folded. Zach watched the marble floor rush up to greet him. As darkness dropped, he thrust his hands out to break his fall. Light-headed and on the floor, he looked at Tufts next to him.

Before Zach passed out, he thought, "Great. Second guy I slept next to in one day."

———

Zora wanted to run up the stairs, she truly did. Instead, she hauled herself up, one step at a time, using the wooden banister as a crutch. Sweating, miserable, panting. Spine on fire. Heart hammering as she heard her brother tussling with Tufts below. Losing precious time and the element of surprise. But she couldn't stop. Not now. Zach could handle himself.

The double bedroom doors were closed. In no mood to knock, she reached for the knobs. The statute of limitations on good manners had long passed. Slowly, she twisted the knob. Then a tiny click sounded behind the doors, barely audible.

"Whoa!" Zora rolled to the side, flattened against the wall. Semi-flattened, actually.

Crack, crack, crick...

Three bullets exited the door, leaving splintered holes as their calling card. Zora waited, listening. No movement. Just wood settling in the door. She turned over on her back. Gun up. Ready.

"You may as well come in. I'm out of bullets," called out Mrs. Turlington.

Yeah, right.

Zora dropped in a squat, hoping she'd be able to pull out of it in time. Reached for the doorknob again.

Shack, crick, splack!

Another volley of bullets broke the wood just above her head. A strand of hair flew up from the rush of the projectiles. She duck-walked back beside the doors. Playing the waiting game again. Nothing. The seconds crawled into minutes.

Now she probably is really out of bullets. I hope.

The doors were pretty much destroyed. Zora peeked through one of the golf ball sized holes. With her back turned toward Zora, Mrs. Turlington stood in front of the same window she'd reigned over this morning. Holding the most elegant gun Zora'd ever seen perched on her hip. A wine glass occupied her other hand. Woman could put the drink away.

Zora entered, gun locked in rigid arms.

"Turn around, Mrs. Turlington! I'm seriously pissed off! I'm hormonal! I feel like a human piñata! And I think I might've just piddled myself a little bit."

Mrs. Turlington turned, smiling ever so diplomatically. "I see you have a gun now. Something I'm sure you didn't have earlier, Mrs. LeFevre."

"Great. You know who I am. Wonderful for you. Soon sucks to be you."

"Of course I know who you and your brother are, dear. I knew it this morning during our visit. I knew it late last night when I hired poor Mr. Martin."

"And then killed him."

"Oh, dear. Things do happen, I suppose. But his usefulness was over to me. Poor delusional man tried to extort me after he'd made a deal with you. Can't have that. Such an immoral world. So as soon as I was off the phone with the late Mr. Martin, I sent Tufty to meet with the detective. Tufty had to move fast. But surely you've realized by now, Tufty's much more than a mere political advisor."

"Why'd you hire Martin?"

"Isn't it obvious? To follow you and your idiotic brother. Find out what you've been up to. You two have been making things exceptionally hard today."

"Why didn't you just call the police on us earlier?"

"Because that would implicate me in my husband's murder."

"You admit to killing him? Your husband?"

"Between you and me, I suppose I do. Won't hold up in court, though. Not when I've killed the two true killers for breaking into my house. Assaulting me with a gun."

"That doesn't sound like a very likely scenario from where I'm standing. Hello! Pissed off pregnant lady holding a damn big gun on you!"

"Let's not put the cart before the horse. How do you know I don't have a contingency plan? What makes you think I won't shoot you?"

"You already decorated your home with six bullets. I think you're out."

She looked at her gun, tilted her head. "Perhaps. Perhaps not. And I certainly wouldn't discount Tufty just yet."

"I would. My brother's got some mad fighting skills."

"So does Tufty."

"'Tufty.' He your lover? That how you got him to go along with the murder of your husband? And Martin?"

"Oh, my, don't be a silly girl! Tufty would like to, ahem, be my lover, I know. But I'm afraid I don't return his affections."

"Then why kill your husband?"

"Because he cheated on me." Her face darkened, rage in her eyes. "Bastard cheated on me. I found out. Actually Tufty did, but no matter. With a more than eager Tufty in tow, we followed Hal's little tart last night. What we found was much better than what I'd initially planned. Too good to be true, a gift from God."

"Yeah, I doubt God had much to do with it."

"Probably not. But I would've been a fool not to act on it."

Zora's arms shook from holding the gun, her muscles weakening. The strain on her back grew, painful. A helluva time for baby to make his presence known. But she couldn't let Mrs. Turlington know that. Sometimes, posturing wins the day.

121

"Alright. Let's end this farce. Come with me. We'll let the police work it out."

Mrs. Turlington laughed. Had the gall to take a large gulp of wine. "I think not. If you believe I'm going that easily, you don't know me very well."

"Can't say as I've had the pleasure of knowing you." Zora released one of her arms, parlaying the strength into her gun-wielding one. She pulled back the trigger. "Would you like to meet my friend, Mr. Bullet? It's happy hour!"

Mrs. Turlington set her glass down on a table. Her arm raised, the gun pointed at Zora.

Crap.

Zora rolled to the side, crashed into a small table.

Zwick. Spwack!

The bullet missed Zora's head by inches. She swung her gun back up, returned fire. The bullet didn't come close to her target, cracking into the window. Glass shattered. Mrs. Turlington groaned, a display of grief over her destroyed window. She tossed her gun at Zora.

Now she's out of bullets, dammit!

Zora wobbled toward her enemy. She needed Mrs. Turlington alive. Less muss, less fuss. Mrs. Turlington ran toward the bed, shouting, "Tufty! Tufty!"

Zora knew she'd regret it, did it anyway. She flung her body onto the older woman, thankful for the bed's cushioned landing pad. Fingers caught into Zora's hair, tugging. Fingernails clawed at her arms. She smacked the woman with the gun. Too hard. The impact bounced the weapon to the floor. Shocked, Zora sat up, looking over the bed for the gun. The older woman grabbed Zora's hair, pulling her back to the bed. Mrs. Turlington crawled over Zora, scrambling for the gun. Zora brought up her hands, hammered them onto Mrs. Turlington's back.

"Oomph."

Mrs. Turlington's head dropped over the bed. Zora climbed down her back, her shoulders. Tucked herself into a sitting position on the floor. Picked up the gun. The baby kicked her an internal high five.

She pressed the gun to the still dazed Mrs. Turlington's silver-haired head. "Are we finished playing?" She huffed the words out between heavy breaths.

"You've got nothing on me. My reputation's golden. You're nothing but an intruder."

"Oh yeah? Wonder how golden your confession's gonna sound on my phone." Totally unnecessary, but Zora played her a few lines anyway. A trick she picked up from the earlier bimbo.

Zach raced in, caught himself on the jagged door.

"Damn, sis! You all right?"

"Your timing sucks, Zach."

"That's not what the ladies think."

For a split second, Zora considered shooting her brother. Maybe just winging him in the leg.

Zora met her brother in the KCMO police parking lot. He looked as tired as she felt.

"Well…that wasn't so bad, sis."

"Speak for yourself."

"Did you give up the lovely Selena Darkly?"

"You better believe I did! She racked up more crimes than we did today. Cops are on their way to pick her up now. Unless she and Dennis have blown town already. They'll get 'em soon enough."

"Right." But Zach didn't look so right, staring down at his feet, kicking a pebble. Forlorn over the one who got away. *Idiot men.* "Anyway, I think I passed with flying colors. They want to ask me more questions tomorrow, though."

"It's typical. Nothing to worry about. We're in the clear. It helps that I still have friends on the force. And Mrs. Turlington's confession, of course."

"Hey, that female detective who grilled me?" Zach whistled. "I'd like to grill—"

Smack.

"Dammit. I thought we'd moved on from that, Zor!"

"And I hope you move on from your silly groin-based life. Honestly! Haven't you learned your lesson?"

"What? What lesson? None of this was my fault!"

Simply impossible. He'll never learn.

"You might want to reconsider that thought."

Briefly, it looked like her brother reconsidered. Nope, he still had nothing.

"Seriously, Zach, why is your big woman-chasing, hetero persona so important to you?"

He leaned up against a cop car. His smile dropped. Letting his guard down for once. "I guess...I guess it's because I feel inferior sometimes..."

"Inferior? To what?"

"Well, to you for one thing."

"Me?"

"Yep, you. You handled this with your usual confidence, your smarts, your wits. Never once did you lose faith in me."

"Oh whatever." She smacked him, this time not so hard and on the shoulder. "Remember, it was you who protected me throughout high school. From the mean girls, the bullies..."

"Yeah, you never did know how to play with people nicely."

"You like how I played with them today?"

"Heh. Guess I did. You were amazing."

"I was, wasn't I?"

"But enough about you, let's talk about me—"

"And you just lost me. You're all we ever talk about."

"Hey. Come here." He pulled her into an embrace. "Thank you. For everything today."

"Don't go getting all sensitive male on me right now, Zach! Hormonally challenged here."

"Really, though, thanks. I couldn't have done it without you."

"Damn straight."

She hugged him tighter. At least as tight as she could from a foot or so distance. Before tears started flowing, she pushed him away.

"You wanna come over, have a celebratory drink? Of the non-roofie type?"

"Is Phillip home?"

"Yep. Probably pitching a fit about now."

"No thanks."

"I'm gonna have to have a long talk with him anyway."

Full-time babysitter, he learns to cook, I'm going back to work. And, oh yeah, that little thing about a mandatory vasectomy…

"Good luck with that."

"Thanks."

"Tell him I'll get his suit back to him tomorrow."

She stood back, definitely downwind, examining the state of her husband's late suit. "Keep it."

A cop approached, asked if they were the brother and sister who needed a ride home.

"Yep."

Zach crawled into the car next to her. Asleep on her shoulder before they left the parking lot. With a tender touch, she caressed his hair and smiled down at her biggest child.

Look for the next Zach and Zora comic mystery:

MURDER BY MASSAGE

About the Author

Stuart R. West is a lifelong resident of Kansas, which he considers both a curse and a blessing. It's a curse because…well, it's Kansas. But it's great because…well, it's Kansas. Lots of cool, strange and creepy things happen in the Midwest, and Stuart takes advantage of them in his work. Call it "Kansas Noir." Stuart writes thrillers, suspense and horror, both for adult and young adult audiences. Stuart spent twenty-five years in the corporate sector and now writes full time. He's married to a professor of pharmacy (who greatly appreciates the fact he cooks dinner for her every night) and has a twenty-six-year-old daughter who's still deciding what to do with her life. But that's okay. It took him twenty-five years to figure that out.

Curious about other Crossroad Press books? Stop by our website:
http://crossroadpress.com
We offer quality writing
in digital, audio, and print formats.

Subscribe to our newsletter on the website homepage and receive a
free eBook.

www.ingramcontent.com/pod-product-compliance
Lightning Source LLC
Chambersburg PA
CBHW022031170626
46808CB00003B/1140